THE FERRYBOAT

When Judy and Tom Jeffrey are asked by their daughter Holly and her Scottish chef husband Corin if they will join them in buying the Ferryboat Hotel in the West Highlands, they take the plunge and move north. The rundown hotel needs much expensive upgrading, and what with local opposition to some of their plans — and worrying about their younger daughter, left down south with her flighty grandma — Judy begins to wonder if they've made a terrible mistake . . .

Books by Kate Blackadder
in the Linford Romance Library:

THE FAMILY AT FARRSHORE

KATE BLACKADDER

◆

THE FERRYBOAT

Complete and Unabridged

LINFORD
Leicester

First published in Great Britain in 2014

First Linford Edition
published 2015

A catalogue record for this book is available
from the British Library.

ISBN 978–1–4448–2657–9

Published by
F. A. Thorpe (Publishing)
Anstey, Leicestershire

Set by Words & Graphics Ltd.
Anstey, Leicestershire
Printed and bound in Great Britain by
T. J. International Ltd., Padstow, Cornwall

This book is printed on acid-free paper

1

After her restless night Judy Jeffrey felt half asleep, and the air coming through the kitchen window was doing nothing to help, being mostly wafts of petrol fumes from the morning rush hour. Living on a busy road was great for passing trade for the B&B but not so good for an incipient headache. And as the planes roared overhead she was acutely reminded of the fact that she lived below the flight path that connected Luton with distant places.

'OK, table three, two bacon and eggs. One tea, one coffee,' Tom broke into her thoughts. She turned round. 'You all right, love?' her husband asked. 'Table one's down. I'll get his order.'

'Bit of a head, that's all.' Judy moved automatically to the cooker and opened a new packet of bacon rashers. She closed her eyes for a moment. She

1

could probably make breakfast that way, but perhaps it was advisable not to try.

'Mum, what are you doing?' Louise, a whirlwind of long hair, heavy book bag, and green school cardigan half off one shoulder, rushed in and popped a slice of bread in the toaster.

'Bacon. Do you want some?'

'As if. I meant, what are you doing with your eyes shut?'

Judy looked at her younger daughter, rummaging now for the jar of chocolate spread.

'You should eat more at breakfast time. I'm just tired.' *Awake half the night worrying about you*, she might have said, but didn't. 'Sometimes it gets to me, all the traffic noise. It's as if we lived on the runway, not six miles away from it.' She laid the rashers in the hot pan and made an effort to sound more cheerful. 'I was thinking about this village we stopped in when we were with Holly and Corin last month. It was beside a loch, and if you closed your eyes you heard water and birds, that's all. It was so peaceful.'

'Sounds horrendous.' Louise took a huge bite of toast. Round her mouth appeared a circle of chocolate spread as if she were a little girl again and not a seventeen-year-old taller than her mother.

Judy handed her a piece of kitchen roll. 'And the water was so smooth and glassy. We got a little boat across it. The ferryman was a real character. Your dad and him had a good chat; put the world to rights.'

'Judy, the bacon and eggs ready?'

'Almost.' Judy put the rashers on a warm plate in the oven and cracked eggs into the pan. 'Sorry, Tom. I was daydreaming about Lorn. Remember, that place where we got the ferry?'

'Where they were building the bridge? I remember. Come on, love, get a grip. I need table three now but table one doesn't want cooked.'

'Good. And that's everyone ordered?' Judy dished up the bacon and eggs and refilled the kettle. 'I'll see if a cup of tea helps blow away my cobwebs.'

Louise wiped her mouth. 'Brush my teeth and then I'm off.' She stopped by the kitchen door. 'Um, I'm seeing Eddie after school.'

Eddie. The reason Judy was awake half the night.

'Again?' She couldn't help her voice rising. 'But you were going to have tea with your gran.'

'We're doing this art project together. It has to be in by Friday. We'll both have tea with Granmar. Eddie thinks she's cool. Byee!' The hair and school-bag and green cardigan disappeared.

'It wasn't an art project that kept you out last night,' Judy said to the kitchen wall. 'That new music venue seems harmless enough, but midnight is far too late to be out mid-week.'

'Talking to yourself?' Tom came in, his hands full of dirty dishes.

'Well, at least I listen, unlike our darling daughter. Could you try and have a word? Tell her she can only stay

4

out late at weekends? Honestly, Holly was a doddle of a teenager compared with Louise.'

'We had our moments with her too. What's the problem? Eddie?'

'Eddie's a nice boy. But she should be spending more time at home studying, not out almost every night of the week. And a bit of help around here would be appreciated.'

'She's dead set on being an architect and she knows that won't happen without passing exams. What about asking Marilyn to speak to her? If Louise takes notice of anyone it's your mother.'

Judy snorted as she switched the dishwasher on. 'My mother! She's a fat lot of help. You're only young once, that's her favourite saying.'

'She's young at heart, Marilyn is,' Tom laughed. 'Seventy going on seventeen. But if she was worried about Louise I'm sure she would tell you.'

'I suppose so. Right, I'm going to sit for five minutes with a cuppa. Clear up here. They should all be ready to check out by then, so I'll do that and get the beds done. Have you got the cash-and-carry list?'

Tom patted his pocket. 'Don't do too much. I'll give you a hand with the rooms when I get back. See you in a couple of hours.'

Judy put her hands around her mug of tea. Ever since they got back from that week in Scotland with their elder daughter and her husband, Judy had felt . . . well, she wasn't sure how she felt. Out of sorts. Wishing for a parallel life lived somewhere else. But nothing was going to change except that next year Louise would leave home for university, and in their empty nest would be herself and Tom doing the same old, same old . . .

She closed her eyes again, better to bring to mind the village she'd told Louise about. They'd all driven from Glasgow, where Holly and Corin lived in a tall building called a tenement, out into the country. They'd stopped in

Oban for coffee, then continued up the west coast, the Indian summer day showing Scotland in her golden glory.

They parked near the ferry in Lorn where Corin produced a lovely picnic lunch, complete with waterproof travelling rug to sit on. Then Judy and Tom walked down to the loch and Tom played ducks and drakes on its mirror-like surface. Above them the skeleton shape of the new bridge arched over the water. Holly and Corin wandered off along the shore, hand in hand.

Well, at least she had one daughter she needn't worry about, Judy thought. Holly liked her job as receptionist in a big Glasgow hotel and was blissfully happy with Corin, the Scottish chef she'd met on a holiday flight and married six months ago.

That September week with them had been time out from everyday life. It was only last month, but already it seemed like a distant dream.

2

'Thank you. Hope we'll see you again.' Holly Grainger smiled at the departing customer and turned to answer the phone. 'Good morning, Glasgow Grand, how may I help you?' As she spoke she looked up to see who was pushing the revolving door from the street.

Corin. She'd left him a couple of hours before, about to head off for his jog, and wasn't expecting to see him until after his shift finished late tonight. He was wearing jeans and a white T-shirt and his dark hair was still damp from his shower.

She finished her call, hoping the phone wouldn't ring again immediately.

'How lovely to see you.' She leaned across the reception desk for his kiss. 'Were you missing me?'

'Every minute. This working different shifts is a pain. But I have an idea that would mean we could work together.'

'How?'

'Listen, sweetheart. You'll be busy again in a minute.' Corin unfolded a piece of paper. 'I went online and found this.'

He passed the paper to her. It wasn't a job advert. The heading was 'Hotel for Sale'.

'But . . . '

'It's in Lorn, where we stopped for lunch with your mum and dad. Remember, Tom suggested having lunch in the hotel, in the Ferryboat, before he knew we'd brought a picnic?'

'I remember, but . . . '

'The hotel's for sale. My brain may still be pumping with adrenalin after my run, but I was wondering if we might buy it. Us, and your mum and dad — combine forces. And my parents might chip in on the money side.'

'Corin, that's amazing . . . You'd have your own kitchen.' Holly was aware of customers walking towards her. 'Look, leave the advert with me. I'll phone

Mum and Dad tonight, shall I?'

Corin mouthed another kiss. 'Great. And I'll sound out my parents.' He backed away from the desk. 'See you later.'

Holly smiled at the customers, a calm smile she hoped, belying what was going on in her head.

In theory it was a perfect idea. A small Highland hotel in an idyllic setting. Mum and Dad's experience, with twenty years of running a busy bed-and-breakfast. Her own qualifications in leisure and tourism, and reception-desk experience. And Corin — well, his amazing cooking would certainly bring in the crowds.

She sneaked a look at the advert printout to see the asking price. It seemed a huge amount. They could sell their flat — the flat Corin had owned himself for five years — so it was bound to have gone up in value. What was the B&B worth? Would Mum and Dad want to uproot themselves and come hundreds of miles north? And what about Louise, and Granmar?

Corin's parents, Verity and Philip, were well-off and, as their only child, Corin was probably right in saying that they would help. But how would that work out? Even after almost a year's acquaintance with her parents-in-law Holly was never very at ease with them. They were very sweet to her but she always had the feeling that they thought Corin could have done better, preferably from among the pool of daughters Philip's solicitor friends seemed to have. And of course they were disappointed that Corin chose not to follow his father into his law firm but instead, in their words, made dinners for a living.

Six hours later she let herself into the empty flat at the top of the tall sandstone building. She went to close the curtains and stood for a moment watching as lights were switched on, like a circuit board coming to life. She liked living in Glasgow but, looking ahead, if she and Corin ever had children she wouldn't want to bring them up in the middle of a city or carry them up three hundred steps after every outing.

Not that babies were on the agenda any time soon. Especially if they were going to have their very own business. She picked up the phone.

'Mum?' As always Holly felt a pang that Mum and Dad were so far away.

'Darling! I've been thinking about you and Corin and that lovely holiday.'

'Great minds. Actually, that's why I'm phoning.'

'You sound ... I don't know, breathless. Is everything all right?'

Holly steadied her voice. 'Mum, do you remember when we got the boat across Loch Lorn? The hotel by the ferry is for sale and Corin thinks we should buy it, go into business together — him and me, and you and Dad. It would be wonderful, wouldn't it? What do you think?'

3

'Why am I the last to know?' Iris Anderson brandished the *Lochaber Herald* in front of her employer. 'I knew it was coming, but why didn't you tell me? Roberta showed me the paper when I dropped Angus off. She says it's on the paper's website too. I couldn't believe — '

Charlie Mack held up both his hands. 'I'm sorry, Iris. I kept putting it off. I was going to tell you this morning, I really was. Trust Roberta to get in first.'

'Don't blame Roberta. I was here yesterday. You could have said something then. Or weeks ago, whenever you decided to sell.'

Charlie sat down at the kitchen table and indicated for Iris to do the same. 'I'm sorry,' he said again. 'I couldn't have carried on as long as I have without you, Iris. I'll tell whoever buys the place what a good worker you are, turn your hand to anything. But the bank has said enough is enough. Or words to that effect. So after sixty years I'm afraid the Ferryboat will go out of the Mack family.' He seemed to age in front of Iris's eyes. Her heart softened.

She got up and put the kettle on. Charlie was like an engine out of fuel unless he had a large mug of strong coffee first thing. 'I didn't know things were that bad,' she said gently, sitting down again. 'Have you . . . ' She hesitated. 'Have you spoken to Sandy?'

Charlie looked startled. 'Sandy?'

'I just wondered,' Iris said. 'Or is he too much the big shot these days to remember his roots?'

Charlie shook his head. 'Sandy's not like that. But no, I haven't told him. Not that we're in regular touch anyway. He phoned a couple of months ago and we had a good yarn, but I kept my troubles to myself.'

Iris was torn between exasperation

and understanding that Charlie's pride would not let him ask for help of any kind. Sandy Mack. Charlie's nephew and only close relative. The last Iris heard of him he was doing whatever he did, his computer wizardry, at some IT company in Zurich. Surely he would want to help to keep the Ferryboat in the family after all these years?

'Is he still in Switzerland?' she asked.

Charlie must have followed her train of thought. 'He was when I spoke to him, but don't you be telling tales. It's not only money that's needed to keep the old Ferryboat afloat; it's energy, youth, imagination . . . All of which Sandy's got. But he's never been interested in the hotel business — you know that. But of course,' Charlie added slyly, 'if you want to get in touch with him for yourself, warm up cold soup . . . '

Iris wrinkled her nose at him. 'Very cold soup that would be,' she said. 'Water under the new Lorn bridge, Charlie.'

The summer after she'd left school she and Sandy had a brief — well, embryonic — romance might be the best way of putting it. As usual she'd come up to Lorn in the holidays to stay with Great-Aunt Janet, and had got a job helping in the Ferryboat kitchen. Sandy was there, odd job man for his Uncle Charlie. They'd had a lot of laughs that summer, and a few kisses when Sandy walked her back to the cottage. But then Fin appeared in her life and swept her away . . . It seemed a lifetime ago, but it was only six years. Now Fin had gone and she was left a widow with her precious little Angus. And Sandy had flown onwards and upwards and turned into a rich whiz kid. They would have nothing to say to each other even if he did come back.

'Pity,' Charlie said, getting up to switch the kettle off. 'You could do with getting a bit of a life for yourself, Iris, whether it's rekindling old flames or something else.'

'I was going to make the coffee,' Iris

protested, but she stayed in her seat as Charlie heaped dessertspoons of his favourite blend into a cafetiere. 'Don't change the subject, Charlie. The hotel's for sale. What are you planning to do with yourself?'

'Haven't thought beyond my armchair and the sports channel.' Charlie put two mugs on the table. 'Let's draw up a plan of action. No guests booked in this week, so we'll have time for a bit of a spruce-up before we get prospective buyers. If we do,' he added gloomily.

'A bit of a spruce-up' was optimistic, Iris thought. A complete makeover was required. But the next owners would have their own ideas on decoration, their own plans — she could only hope that those plans would include herself, Charlie's only full-time member of staff in the low season.

Slumped in his chair, her employer looked less a man of action and more like a teddy bear that was losing its stuffing.

'Right,' she said briskly. The future of the Ferryboat might not involve Iris Anderson, but she was here to work now. 'Could you tidy the office? It's a tip. I'll start on the kitchen cupboards and the store-room. And I've had a thought. How about if I ask Roberta to lend some of her tubs, cheer up round the front door?' She stood up and reached for her overall. 'Come on, Mr Mack, let's get sprucing.'

★ ★ ★

'Tubs? Could do. Although why, I don't know. Lazy old buzzard's let the place go. Told him that. Now he comes crawling.'

Iris grinned, not fooled by Roberta's diatribe. Her friend's brusque ways hid the proverbial heart of gold.

'It was my idea, not Charlie's,' she said. 'I thought it would create a good initial impression.'

'Good initial impression, yes. Not

prepare them for the rack and ruin inside though.'

Angus climbed onto Iris's knee. 'What's rackandruin, Mummy?'

Iris cuddled him. 'One of Robbie's favourite expressions. Where the whole world is headed, apparently.' She blew a raspberry into Angus's ear. 'Nothing for you to worry about, my pet. OK, let's go. Your Auntie Lizzie will be home soon.' She looked at Roberta. 'Thanks. Don't know what I'd do without you. Angus loves coming here.'

When Iris's last child-minder moved away, Roberta, retired early from teaching, stepped in. Now that Angus was at school she saw him on and off the bus when necessary and kept him until Iris could pick him up.

'We've been planting daffie bulbs today.' Iris had already guessed that from the state of Angus's fingernails.

Roberta followed them to the front door and gave an exaggerated sigh. 'Since it's you, I'll get Donnie to help lug a couple of tubs up to the 'boat.

Oh, news — Donnie says there's been vandalism on the bridge. Girders damaged or somesuch. Any delay means the ferry will run for longer. Donnie's trying not to smile about it.'

Roberta spoke as if Donnie, the Lorn ferryman for the last twenty years, was a mere acquaintance. Yet she had been engaged to him for the last eleven of those years. Iris had given up trying to understand their relationship, but it seemed to suit them, which was what mattered. Apparently there had been an engagement ring, now lost; but never, as far as Iris knew, a date set for the wedding.

Angus walked backwards so that he could wave to Roberta all the way down the path. Roberta waved back.

'I hope you keep your job,' she called to Iris. 'Who knows what kind of people will end up running the 'boat.'

4

'Oh, I wish we could go,' Judy said for the umpteenth time, gazing in frustration at the computer screen, which showed that the B&B was booked solid for the next two weeks. There was no way that she and Tom could leave it even for a day to go and view the Ferryboat with Holly and Corin.

Tom squeezed her shoulder. 'I know. But they'll get a feel for the place and ask all the right questions. Suss out if it's worth the asking price. But selling up here . . . there's a thought.'

Judy nodded. 'We'll tell Louise and Mother this afternoon but stress that it's only a possibility. Lou should be back about four. That suits Mother — it's between her walking group and her yoga class.'

'Are you finished on the computer?' Tom asked. 'I thought I'd have a look to see what properties in the street are fetching. I hope we're sitting on a goldmine!'

'Corin said his parents would chip in.' Judy stood up to let Tom sit on the office chair.

'Would *invest*. That's how Philip and Verity would see it. And that could mean they'd want some say. Interfere. Or expect to stay for nothing and bring their friends. His golfing *pals*.'

Judy had to laugh. ''Never worry worry 'til worry worries you,'' she quoted. 'Philip's rather overbearing, I agree, but I think I'd get on with Verity if we knew each other better. You're right, though. Their involvement would have to be clear. I'm more concerned about whether there's living accommodation for four people.'

It was Tom's turn to be soothing. 'Holly and Corin will find out about that. It may be all pie-in-the-sky anyway, Judy. Are we having a joint mid-life crisis even considering it?'

'Well, we are in the middle of our

lives if you think about it.' Judy leaned over the chair and put her arms around her husband. 'Our baby will be leaving home next summer. You're going to have a bald spot soon.' She grabbed Tom's hand as it automatically flew to the top of his head, and held it tight. 'I've started to make oofy noises when I sit down. But hey, it's *mid*-life. There's still a long way to go, all things being equal. We don't need to make a crisis out of it. Just a few changes.'

'Buying a hotel four hundred miles away! In Scotland! Just a *few* changes.' Tom kissed her hand. 'Do you know what next door paid for theirs last year? I suppose I could come out with it and ask.'

'I had a thought about them,' Judy said. 'Do you think — '

The phone rang. Tom disengaged his hand to answer it and Judy left him to it and went to finish changing beds.

They hadn't said anything to Louise or to Marilyn about Holly's phone call. But now that things had moved on, and now that Holly and Corin had an appointment to view the hotel, it was time to tell the rest of their family what was in the air.

So Judy was annoyed when Louise breezed in after school and headed straight for the biscuit tin — with Eddie one step behind her.

'Lou, you know your gran will be here in a minute. She's bringing some fancy macaroons from that deli. We, your dad and I, wanted to have a chat with you both.'

'*Macarons*, not macaroooons. There's a difference. Granmar told me. Wow, they were wicked.' Louise put the lid back on the tin. 'She had raspberry and white chocolate ones when we were round the other day — didn't she, Eddie?'

'I mean, we want to have a serious chat with you and Granmar, Louise. We have something to tell you.'

Eddie seemed to get her drift even if Louise didn't. 'That's fine; I'll be off. See you tomorrow, Lou,' he said.

'No, don't go — we were going to download music from that band.' Louise looked at Judy. 'Surely you can say whatever it is in front of Ed?'

'It is a family thing,' Judy started to say, but the unmistakable rattle of Marilyn's old Mini could be heard and she went out to guide her mother into a parking space.

How did she drive in those heels? Judy wondered as Marilyn got out of the car. They must be a good two inches high, maybe more. Her mother wasn't dressed for either walking or yoga. With the shoes she wore smart black trousers and a pink blouse with wide sleeves gathered at the wrist. Her hair and make-up were immaculate.

I meant to change before she came, Judy remembered, looking down at her own jeans and baggy checked shirt. Guiltily, she thought of the top Marilyn had given her for her last birthday, blue and green, in a flattering fitted shape. It was upstairs in her wardrobe, along with the gauzy scarf from Christmas and all the other pretty garments Marilyn wrapped up so beautifully for her ungrateful daughter.

'Macarons!' Marilyn flourished a white box. 'Lemon. Violet. Look too good to eat, but I expect we'll manage.'

Louise swooped on them. 'Oooh, they're gorgeous. Look, Eddie.'

'Can you put them on a plate, Lou, please?' Judy said, making tea. 'Sit down, Mother. Here's Tom now.'

Marilyn acknowledged her son-in-law by blowing him a kiss. 'Goodness. Quite an air of mystery, dear. What's going on?'

It finally seemed to dawn on Louise that her parents had something important to say. She left Eddie's side, came over to the table and popped a whole macaron into her mouth.

Between them, Judy and Tom related the plan so far. 'So,' Tom concluded, 'Holly and Corin are going to view the hotel next week and we'll take it from there.'

Louise almost choked. 'And what

26

about me?' she said when she could speak. 'Have you forgotten that I have my A-levels in a few months? I don't want to go to a new school in the middle of nowhere. Are you kidding?'

'Well, we thought — ' began Judy, but Louise jumped up.

'Eddie, I'm not staying here. Come on.' Eddie looked at Judy apologetically before following Louise out of the kitchen.

Marilyn put down her cup. 'Scotland. How lovely,' she said calmly. 'We honeymooned in Scotland, your father and I. The Isle of Arran. We always said we'd go back one day. Where's your hotel, did you say?'

'By Loch Lorn in Argyllshire,' Judy said. 'But of course we don't want Lou to change schools at this stage. We — '

'Yes,' said Marilyn, helping herself to a violet macaron. 'Of course she can stay with me until she finishes school. We'll have a ball.'

Judy didn't know whether to laugh or to cry. 'That's wonderful. If it happens.

But I don't like the thought of leaving you, Mother. It's so far away.'

Marilyn patted her hand. 'Planes, trains, automobiles. Emails. Phone calls. Texts. And Eddie's told me about Skyping. You need a change, both of you. Change is good. Your father didn't like taking chances, Judy, and look at him — a heart attack before he was fifty. Now, do you think your own place will sell quickly?'

'I was wondering.' Judy looked at Tom and back to her mother. 'Jim next door runs a B&B too, and his wife looked after ours when we were on holiday, remember? I got the impression they were keen to expand.'

'I'll sound Jim out,' Tom said. 'No harm in asking. Any takers for that last lemon one?'

'You help yourself, dear,' said Marilyn, getting out her mobile phone. 'I'll text Louise. Tell her I'm looking for a lodger.'

5

Iris inhaled. Yes, the hotel smelt of freshly made coffee and the sweet aroma of baking. She'd popped the dough in the oven twenty minutes before the prospective buyers were due to arrive and now the biscuits were cooling on a rack.

Last night she'd done something she hoped she wouldn't regret. She'd Googled 'Alexander Mack Zurich'. His name came up on a company website but with no direct email address. So she'd decided to write and tell him what was happening to the Ferryboat and how despondent his uncle seemed to be. Before she could change her mind this morning she'd given the letter to Lizzie to post on her way to work.

She peeped round the office door. The little room looked tidy, but she suspected that all Charlie had done was to stuff into the filing cabinet the mass of papers that had cluttered the desk-top. All that remained was the telephone and the large hardback notebook in which they wrote down bookings.

A pity there was no way of hiding faded wallpaper, or bed linen that was a riot of dated patterns and colours. Still, she thought, as she went to check the dining room, the new owners could take time to replace those, upgrade the whole place; but they'd already have for free the best thing of all — the view here from the picture window. Diners always exclaimed over it.

The hotel garden with its wind-blown trees sloped gently down to the water and the calm silver surface of the loch drew the eye to the houses on the other side. So near and yet so far. She leaned closer to the window and looked at the half-built bridge on her right. Soon the two villages, Lorn and North Lorn, would only be a few minutes apart.

'Iris,' Charlie called from the kitchen, 'they're here.'

She hurried through. 'You meet them at the front door. Mr and Mrs Grainger,' she reminded him before he squared his shoulders and strode off into the hall.

'I'm Corin Grainger and this is my wife, Holly,' Iris heard the newcomer say. She opened the kitchen door a fraction more and caught a glimpse of a dark-haired man and a girl in a stylish red dress. Goodness. They looked younger than herself.

She busied herself counting pieces of cutlery. The solicitors had told Charlie that a complete inventory would be required. Charlie was to take them upstairs first and give them the tour, ending up in the dining room, where they could admire the view and Iris would serve coffee and biscuits.

But when Charlie brought the couple into the kitchen the girl sat down, laying a camera on the table. 'This is Corin's department,' she said with a smile. 'I warn you, he'll leave no cupboard unseen. I'm Holly,' she said, holding out her hand.

'This is Iris,' said Charlie. 'Been working for me on and off since she was a schoolgirl. Extremely reliable. Versatile. Cleaner, receptionist, chambermaid, you name it. And she — '

'Can I get you coffee, Mrs Grainger?' Iris interrupted. Charlie putting in a word for her was one thing. Laying it on with a trowel was another.

'I'd love one. Please call me Holly.' She threw her husband a laughing glance. 'We've only been married six months. I still think of Mrs Grainger as being Corin's mother.' She took a sip of coffee. 'I'm a receptionist in the Glasgow Grand. We've got a computer booking system there but you seem more low-tech here.'

'You could say that,' said Iris, wanting to laugh. There was an ancient laptop somewhere about but Charlie had resisted all her efforts to get him to use it, or to have the hotel website updated.

'Corin's a fabulous chef,' Holly chatted on. 'He'd love to have his own kitchen.'

The 'fabulous chef' was looking rather aghast, no doubt because of the lack of equipment Iris was familiar with from watching *Masterchef*. He came and sat down.

'Great biscuits. You do the cooking here too, Iris?'

Iris looked at Charlie before replying. 'Not cooking as such, no. Baking for morning coffees. We take someone on to cook in the summer months, and now Charlie does it himself.' She didn't say that his 'cooking' consisted mostly of heating frozen fish or scampi with chips for the bridge workers, while resident or passing dinner guests got . . . well, Charlie made good use of the microwave.

She went back to her cutlery and watched the Graingers as they asked Charlie questions and feeling a pang as she saw how happy they seemed, leaning into each other, their eyes bright with their plans for the future. It would be fun to work for them, she thought. *But*. She stopped counting and listened. If they bought it they would be running the hotel with her parents, apparently. At this time of year it could easily be run by four people.

When Fin's car accident coincided with Great-aunt Janet dying and leaving Brook Cottage to herself and her sister Lizzie, it was to Lorn that Iris had fled. Lizzie gave up her flat-share in Oban to come to be with Iris and baby Angus, commuting now to the town by bus. She hated that journey, Iris knew, and her job in the bank. After four years Iris felt strong enough to be on her own but Lizzie, her protective elder sister, didn't see that.

But now, how could she manage on her own? The insurance money from the accident was tied up for Angus's future, a decision she'd made at the time and never gave any further thought to. Employment prospects in Lorn were as scarce as roses in

December. She relied on what Charlie paid her. It wasn't much, but then she never went anywhere to spend it.

Charlie had stood up. 'Iris?'

Iris blinked. *Stop feeling sorry for yourself.* She tried to smile at this golden young couple with enough money to buy a hotel.

'Could you show Corin and, er, Holly the annexe? And then we'll finish seeing this floor.'

Iris put down the forks. The annexe had been built for Charlie's parents to live in and was rarely used now. Iris had opened the windows to air it but it looked and felt neglected.

Would the view from the dining room be enough to persuade the Graingers to turn a blind eye to the hotel's deficiencies? She didn't know whether she hoped it would or not.

6

'That kitchen is a joke,' said Corin as they got back into the car. 'The cooker's not much better than a domestic one. And the fridge — '

Holly scrolled through the photographs on her digital camera. 'It could be gorgeous, couldn't it? I've got loads of ideas about colours and fabrics.'

'Tom and Judy will have a fit when they see how much there is to do.'

'I won't send all my photos,' Holly said. 'Mum will love that view from the dining room. And the front looked nice, with those plant tubs.'

''Potential' is definitely the word.' Corin turned to smile at her. 'At least I wouldn't have a hard act to follow here, cooking-wise. The store-room had mostly frozen or microwaveable stuff.'

'You wait a couple of years. That

dining room will be booked from one end of the year to the other. Michelin stars here we come.'

Corin stroked her arm. 'I like your confidence, sweetheart.'

'What are you going to tell Verity and Philip?'

He looked at her, apologetically this time. 'When you went to see the annexe I tried to get some financial details. Our Mr Mack wasn't very forthcoming. I'll get Dad on to it, all the legal stuff. I made an appointment for my parents to come and see the place — Monday afternoon next week.'

Oh no. Did that mean Philip and Verity would swan in and take over? Holly didn't care for the heavy furniture and fussy décor in their house in Edinburgh. She wouldn't want that style imposed on the Ferryboat. And Dad and Philip hadn't exactly hit it off the few times they'd met.

'But — oh I wish my mum and dad were free to come up.' Holly bit her lip.

'It's them who would be living here, not your parents.'

'I know that, Holly. But if we decide to go ahead, we're going to need whatever my father can offer towards the cost. He is a solicitor. You can't expect him to go into this blindly.'

'I know that,' said Holly in her turn. 'I'm not stupid. '*If* we decide to go ahead' — does that mean you didn't like it?'

'My head is bursting with plans,' Corin said tightly, 'but I'm trying to be practical. It's not as easy as buying a new dress.'

Surely they weren't having a row? Holly swallowed. 'Of course Philip and Verity should see it,' she said. 'I wasn't thinking. Shall we come up and see it with them?'

'It's my day off and you're on an early.' Corin sounded like his normal self again. 'I'll pick you up when you finish your shift. Don't worry, Dad's well disposed towards the idea — a new golf course is opening next spring about five miles away. What was that annexe like, by the way?'

He had opted to stay and talk business with Charlie while Iris took Holly to see round the building at the back of the hotel.

'Iris seemed nice, didn't she? A pity we won't need her,' Holly said. 'The annexe has two rooms, plus a bathroom and a tiny kitchen/diner. How would you feel about living with Mum and Dad?'

'Honey, if it goes ahead we'll be too busy to even think about it.' He squeezed her hand.

'Shall we park by the ferry, have a look around the village? Do you think you could settle here, in a small place?'

'I love it,' said Holly. 'I've always wanted to live beside water.'

Corin leaned over for a quick kiss before starting the car.

7

It was Judy's turn to drive and they were almost there.

This is it, Tom thought. *Our new life is just up ahead. No going back.* Certainly he wouldn't want to literally go back now. For the last couple of hours the car had been buffeted by wind and now Judy had to slow to a crawling pace because of the fog. There couldn't be more of a contrast with that mellow September day when they'd picnicked by the loch-side.

But it wasn't a bad omen. It was just weather, normal for the end of January.

The last three months blurred together in his memory. Holly and Corin had glowed with such enthusiasm over their plans for putting the hotel on the map that Tom and Judy put up a No Vacancies sign for a day and flew from Luton to Glasgow, where

Corin had driven them up to see the Ferryboat. Back home, encouraged by Marilyn, they'd agreed to put in an offer.

Philip Grainger came on board, as he put it. Corin's flat was sold. Jim next door put in a good offer for the B&B. Louise and Marilyn expressed themselves very happy with their new living arrangements. Now Judy and Tom's furniture was somewhere on the road behind them and Holly and Corin were waiting for them in Lorn, having gone up yesterday as soon as they got the keys.

Tom smiled grimly to himself. All they had to do now was make the Ferryboat viable and not lose stonking amounts of money for everyone concerned.

The car turned into the short drive in front of the hotel. As Judy drew up to park there was a rather sickening thud.

'Judy!' Tom expostulated. 'That sounded expensive. Must be a pothole.'

'I was on it before I realised. Sorry,

Tom.' Judy sounded stricken.

Tom sighed. 'So, we've got a car park that needs resurfacing. Hope we won't need a mechanic as well.' He looked around. 'Can't see their car. Wonder where they've gone?'

Judy clutched his arm. 'One of them must be here. Look, smoke's coming from that chimney. A real fire! And some of Corin's cooking to look forward to. We'll have a lovely evening, the four of us, before the hard work begins.'

'Here's Holly,' Tom said as the back door opened. He got out of the car.

'Oh, Dad.' Holly ran towards him. 'Do you know anything about fires? I can't get it to light properly — the whole room's full of smoke.'

Tom headed inside, gesturing to Judy to follow him.

'I wanted everything to be nice for you and Mum.' Holly was on the verge of tears. 'I've made up a couple of beds and unpacked some of our stuff. And someone had put paper and sticks in the fireplace in the sitting-room and I found some matches, but . . . '

She had not exaggerated. Tom coughed as he made his way to the fireplace.

'If someone made up the fire it suggests it's in regular use.' Judy stood in the doorway, an arm round Holly. 'So it won't be that the chimney needs cleaning.'

'Your mother's right,' Tom said to Holly. 'The wind will be blowing down the chimney. Your fire didn't have a chance to catch properly. Look, I'll put this guard in front of it. We'll open the window just a little bit. There. Close the door.' He stood in the corridor, clearing his throat.

'Phew. Welcome to the Ferryboat.' He gave Holly a kiss. 'Where's Corin?'

This time Holly's eyes did brim over. 'He went to do some food shopping — but that was hours ago, and he's not answering his mobile.'

Tom looked at Judy and raised his eyebrows. 'Hey,' he said gently. 'It's not like there's a supermarket on the doorstep. And it's so misty out there he'll be driving really slowly.' Then, feeling that by mentioning the bad driving conditions he'd given Holly something else to worry about, he hastened to add, 'Come on, let's explore at our leisure. Our visit was so rushed.'

Holly rubbed her eyes, led the way into the room on the other side of the corridor and switched on the light. 'My favourite room.'

Tom saw a room hung with patterned green wallpaper and bland flower prints. Hmm, well, not to his taste but if Holly liked it . . .

'Grim, isn't it?' Holly said. 'Like a doctor's waiting room. But the view is brilliant.' She crossed to the window. 'Oh no!'

Tom and Judy joined her. All they could see was the reflections of their three selves and the room behind them. Tom pressed his face to the glass. Possibly that was a tree, but then again it might be a telegraph pole. Or a very tall Scotsman. He turned back to his wife and daughter.

'Shall we save the tour for the morning? Tomorrow is another day, as the woman said.'

Judy laughed. 'And she was right. Listen, what's that noise?'

'Corin!' Holly rushed into the hall, and then stopped. Someone was knocking on the front door.

'Who — ?'

Tom walked past her and undid the bolts. He peered into the gloom.

A middle-aged lady stood uncertainly on the step. 'I wasn't sure if there was anyone in,' she said. 'I've missed the last ferry and I don't want to drive round the loch in the mist. Do you have a bed for the night?'

8

Miss Fisher turned out to find the whole situation very amusing. She even offered to make up a bed for herself if that would be any help.

Thank goodness she came, Judy thought, as Holly took their guest upstairs, Tom following with her suit-case. *She's distracted Holly from worrying about Corin and made us remember why we're here. Maybe even stopped us from falling out with each other.*

Judy wandered through the ground floor, looking into rooms, opening cupboard doors, feeling as if she was snooping in someone else's house. *I live here now,* she reminded herself. But it didn't feel like home, and the gloom outside didn't help. She drew all the curtains, then headed for the kitchen.

In the store-room there were tins and

packets they could make a meal from tonight if for some reason Corin hadn't managed to buy any supplies. Miss Fisher would surely not want to eat alone in the chilly dining-room, so Judy rummaged until she found a tablecloth and cutlery and set the large kitchen table for five. She pulled the blinds down, then imagining Corin seeing the place in darkness, opened them again and found an outside light she switched on.

'Don't know what's wrong with the heating,' Tom said, startling her. 'I'll check it out in the morning. I've found one of those Calor gas heaters in a back room. I'll bring it through here.'

'Where're Holly and Miss Fisher?'

'Still upstairs, chatting away. Miss F knows the area.'

'I think her night with us should be on the house,' said Judy, 'what with everything at sixes and sevens. And it looks as if I'll just be throwing a pasta dish together for us all if Corin's not back soon.'

47

'Agreed, definitely,' said Tom. 'What she must have thought, when the door opened and three folk were gawping at her as if she were the ghost of Christmas past. I'll get that heater.'

'Mum . . . ' Holly passed Tom in the kitchen doorway. 'What shall I do with Miss Fisher? The sitting-room's like a morgue. Talk about Highland hospitality!'

'Bring her in here,' Judy said. 'This is going to be the warmest room tonight.'

Holly picked up her mobile from the work surface and put it down again. 'Nothing from Corin.'

'Don't worry, darling. Go and ask Miss Fisher if she'd like to come down and join us.'

Looking at Holly's phone reminded Judy that she should call Marilyn and Louise to say that they'd arrived safely. Everything was lovely, she would tell them. The gory details of the weather and all the work there was to do could wait. As she went to find her handbag for her mobile she could hear a telephone ringing.

The landline. Where on earth was it? She ran through the ground floor listening at doors, finally running it to earth in a small room near the front door.

'The Ferryboat, good evening,' she said breathlessly, part of her mind wondering how many times she was going to say that, or some variation of it, in the years to come.

'We would like,' a voice said, in an accent she couldn't place, 'to come to your lovely hotel for dinner tonight. We have heard such good things about the new chef. There will be ten of us.'

It was flattering that news had travelled about Corin — but accommodating Miss Fisher was one thing; this was impossible. And who would want to be out on such a night?

'I'm so sorry,' Judy began, 'I'm afraid . . . '

'It's Philip, Judy. Got you!' Philip spoke in his normal voice and roared with laughter.

'You've arrived then?'

'Philip.' Judy sank onto the old swivel chair behind the table. Not her idea of a joke, but it had been a long day. And he was Corin's father and a sleeping partner in the business. 'Ha ha! Yes, here we are. Everything's going well.' She crossed her fingers. 'We arrived about an hour ago. The weather's pretty bad but we're looking forward to seeing the place in daylight tomorrow.'

'Dreich, is it, Judy? That's a good Scots word for describing dreary weather. And you'll get plenty of that on the west coast I expect. W for west, w for wet and wild. Corin about?'

Does it never rain in Edinburgh? Judy wondered. Honestly. 'He's gone food shopping,' she said, trying to keep her voice upbeat. 'We're expecting him back any minute.'

'Good, good. Ask him to give me a bell. How is my lovely daughter-in-law? What is it?' asked Philip, evidently addressing the last question to someone at his end. 'Yes, all right. Verity says

50

she's thinking of you and I've to leave you to get settled in.'

'Give her my love. I'll get Corin to ring you.' Judy hung up.

'Who on earth was that?' Tom popped his head round the door.

'Philip.'

'Checking up on us already, was he?'

'Something like that. I'll give Mum and Louise a quick call. See you in a minute.'

When she got back to the kitchen Tom and Miss Fisher were sitting at the table, and Holly stood beside her father flicking her fingers over her mobile phone.

'This is all looking very homely, Mrs Grainger,' Miss Fisher said. 'I do appreciate it.'

'Not quite the welcome we'd envisaged for our first guest,' Judy said. 'It's good of you to take us as you find us.'

As her mind went to concocting something edible if not sophisticated for dinner, car lights beamed through the kitchen window. 'Corin.' Holly ran to open the back door. Her husband came in, several carrier bags in each hand.

'Sorry. Hope you weren't worried,' he said, giving Holly a kiss. 'Got talking to the owner of a deli. He's given me names of lots of local suppliers. A smokery. A seafood place. And I found a great butcher.' He started to unpack the bags. 'Venison steaks sound good for tonight? I got enough to feed an army.'

'Good. We're five now. This is Miss Fisher,' Tom said.

'I blew in with the wind,' Miss Fisher laughed. 'Venison steaks sound wonderful.'

Indeed they did. With a lighter heart Judy went to pull down the blinds and shut out the storm.

9

She knew she should leave it for a day or two before visiting the Ferryboat, but Roberta couldn't resist going up on Saturday, the day after the new owners moved in.

To make it look as if she wasn't just being curious (a polite word for nosy, she'd always thought), she picked up a jar of the rowan jelly she made every year. She could take it as a present and ask this wonderful new chef if he'd be interested in buying some. Actually, that would be a good idea, come to think of it. Even after giving lots away she still had more than she could use. She added another jar to her bag.

As she rang the bell in the Ferryboat's reception area, she thought how much nicer the front entrance had looked with her tubs of fuchsias one on either side of the door.

A woman came through from the back; a bit younger than herself, and pleasant-looking. 'Good morning.'

'Good morning.' Roberta held out her hand. 'I'm Roberta Roberts. I know. What were my parents thinking? It's a long story. Another time. I live down the road, the cottage with the green gate.'

The woman shook her hand, her expression still friendly but her eyes rather dazed. 'Judy Jeffrey. Good to meet you.'

'I came to say hello, welcome, and I brought you some rowan jelly.' Roberta took the jars out of her bag and laid them on a side table, wishing now she'd taken time to pretty them up a bit, cloth cover maybe, fancy writing on the label. Oh well, too late now.

'How nice of you,' Judy said. 'Come in and meet the rest of the family. Well, Tom and Holly are in the annexe — our own furniture is arriving today and it will have to go in there — but Corin, our son-in-law, is here.'

'We're all expecting great things from your son-in-law,' Roberta said. 'Put Lorn on the map, will he?' As they walked through to the kitchen, she covertly looked around so that she could report any changes to Iris. But of course the new owners hadn't had a chance to make any yet. The only thing of note was a strong smoky smell.

'Did you try to light a fire in the sitting-room last night?' she asked.

Judy looked at her as if she was Miss Marple.

'Don't, not when the wind is in the east. It goes right down the chimney,' Roberta advised. In the kitchen she looked with interest at Corin who, sleeves rolled up, was cleaning out the fridge. 'It will be good to have someone who can cook around here. Poor old Charlie did his best, mind, but you don't get Michelin stars for fish and chips. Now, I can see you're up to your eyes. Need a hand?'

Judy looked taken aback.

'Not me,' Roberta guffawed. 'No, I

was thinking of Iris. Worked here on and off since she was a kid.'

'We heard about Iris,' Judy said. 'Holly and Corin met her. But there are four of us sorting things out before the decorators come in. I think we'll manage.'

Well, she'd tried. 'Leave you to it then.' Roberta declined Judy's offer of coffee, sensing it was polite rather than heartfelt. In the hall she noticed the rowan jelly on the table. Rats. She'd forgotten to mention it to the chef.

'Can you recommend somewhere nearby where we could buy some planters?' Judy asked as she showed Roberta out. 'When we came to view there were fuchsias in lovely half-barrels here by the door. I've no idea what happened to them.'

'Hmm.' If Judy had been able to peer into Roberta's little greenhouse she would see those very items. 'There's a garden centre near Oban. Grant's Gardening World. They're in the phone book.'

'Thank you. And thanks for coming, Roberta,' Judy said. 'Next time I hope you'll stay for longer.' She did sound as if she meant it.

Yesterday's stormy sky was diluted to watery blue today, and the waves on Loch Lorn, although white-edged, were not preventing the ferry from running. Roberta shaded her eyes and squinted. She could just make out Donnie on the deck. Too far away for him to see her if she waved.

At Brook Cottage Angus and Iris were picking up leaves from the pocket-handkerchief front lawn.

'Ooh, I want those,' Roberta said as Angus lifted up a foot to show off his new red wellies.

'Come in,' Iris said, 'Lizzie and I were just going to have coffee.'

Lizzie and Iris didn't look like sisters. Iris was — well, rather like an iris. Rather delicate and fair. Lizzie was dark-haired and larger. She looked rather fierce until she smiled, which she did now.

'You look as if you're bearing news, Robbie.'

Roberta threw herself into the armchair nearest the fire. 'Not much,' she said. 'Paid a neighbourly visit to the Ferryboat. Seem nice enough people. But no go, Iris. You'd've thought that old goat Charlie would have said you were part of the package.'

'Oh, I wish you . . . but thanks for trying,' said Iris. 'They've no legal obligation to keep me on. Something will turn up.' She glanced at Roberta and then at Angus. Roberta took the hint and changed the subject.

After leaving Brook Cottage, Roberta went back to her own house where she made up sandwiches, put them in a paper bag and took them down to the ferry along with a flask of coffee. Donnie was jumping ashore to tie up the boat.

'Lunch,' Roberta said.

'Cheers.' Donnie stuffed the bag and the flask into his oilskin pockets. 'How's things?'

'Met the new folk at the 'boat. They — '

'I have too,' Donnie said. 'Well, I've met Tom. He was out for a walk first thing. Seems a good bloke. He told me we've actually spoken before — they got the ferry last September.' He tied the final knot. 'They're going to try and keep the bar open because of the bridge workers, but otherwise they'll be closed until the end of March.'

'You did find out a lot,' Roberta said, annoyed that she had no information to pass on.

'Must go,' Donnie said, as cars started to come off the ferry. He tipped his yellow sou'wester back and leaned forward to smack a kiss on her cheek. 'Thanks for the sandwiches.' He looked towards the Ferryboat and grinned. 'I've no doubt, Ro, you'll find out everything there is to know before long.'

10

This will be our first married Valentine's Day, was Holly's first thought when she woke up. She put out her hand to find Corin but the other side of the bed was empty.

They had the biggest bedroom for the moment, the one above the dining room, with the view over the loch. It would be gorgeous when it was decorated in the creamy yellow scheme she'd planned, especially when the morning light filtered through the curtains. She would be sorry when the annexe was refurbished for the four of them to move into.

Downstairs Corin, dressed in shorts, was drinking a glass of water. 'I tried not to wake you, sweetheart,' he said to her. 'I haven't been for a run for ages. Must get into the habit again.'

Holly gave him a small smile. *No,* she

told herself, *don't mention Valentine's Day*. Besides, her mum and dad were here, eating cereal at the table. Holly got a bowl for herself and sat down.

'What are we all doing today then?' Dad asked. 'Judy and I are going to tackle the annexe.'

Their furniture from the B&B had been stuffed into the annexe, along with what Corin and Holly had taken from their Glasgow flat. Before they had any chance to paint the place, never mind move in, they had to decide what to keep for their own use and what to put in the hotel.

'I'll give you a hand after I've spoken to the painter,' Holly said. 'He's coming at half eight. And Corin and I will do the bar lunches.'

Corin sat down beside her. 'Now that I've spoken to some suppliers and know what I can get, I'll start to plan menus. We could offer dinners before the bedrooms are ready, couldn't we?'

Dad nodded. 'Great idea. Start the ball rolling. I'll do a notice and try to get some publicity,' he said.

'The painter's starting with the downstairs cloakroom,' Holly said. She put her bowl in the dishwasher. 'Oh, I know what else I've got to do. That book-in book Charlie Mack showed us. I'll go through the office yet again, see if I can find it. I wish we were getting the computer system in place before next month.'

She was in the office when Philip rang. Since that first phone call the night they'd arrived he hadn't put on any silly voices when he phoned, but he did call fairly regularly to 'check up on them' as Dad put it, though not in front of Corin of course.

He and Verity had made a flying visit a few weeks ago. It would have to be the day when most of the ground floor had had its wallpaper stripped off and the furniture was covered in dustsheets. Even Verity had looked aghast, but Corin had made a fabulous dinner that Philip said was worth travelling to the Wild West for.

'How's my favourite daughter-in-law?' Philip asked now.

Holly laughed dutifully.

'Now, we've been talking at the golf club. We'd like to make a booking at the Ferryboat for the first week in May. That's when the new golf course opens at Benlorn. Four twin rooms. For yours truly plus seven pals. Do you need their names?'

Holly tried to sound as professional as if she were at the reception desk of the Glasgow Grand instead of in this poky room scrabbling to find a pen. 'Not at this stage, Philip. I'll put the booking under your name. We'll look forward to seeing you all.'

'You'll see Verity and myself before then of course. Set a date for the big opening party?'

Holly grimaced at the phone. 'Not yet. You'll be the first to know, Philip.' As she hung up she could hear Corin opening the door to the painter.

She couldn't help remembering last Valentine's Day, a few weeks before they got married. Their work shifts had meant that they wouldn't be able to see each other all day. But Corin had turned up at the Grand with a little wicker basket containing some of her favourite things to eat on her lunch break. Underneath she'd found an envelope with a card and a delicate heart-shape on a silver chain.

She remembered what he said in the card, and put up her hand to touch the necklace. She'd worn it every day since, even on their wedding day. She had got Corin a present for this Valentine's Day, bought ages ago before they moved. She'd thought the day would start with a present exchange so his was still hidden upstairs.

'Sweetheart?' Corin pushed open the door of the office. 'Garry's here. He's to do the cloakroom this morning?'

'Yes.' Holly pulled herself together. 'I'm just coming. I still haven't found the book-in book.'

Garry the painter joined them later for a sandwich lunch in the kitchen.

'I've been looking at the hotel sign by the gate,' Dad said. 'I thought it only needed repainting but it's falling to bits. We'll have to get a new one made. So I was wondering . . . ' He looked around the table. ' . . . if we might take the opportunity to change the name?'

'Change the name?' Judy repeated.

'The actual ferryboat won't be running for much longer, will it? How about the Bridge Inn? Garry, you're local. What do you think?'

'You can try,' Garry said, grinning.

'I'll go ahead then,' said Dad. 'The Bridge Inn. Sounds good, I think.'

After an afternoon spent moving furniture about in the annexe, Holly went back to the hotel and had a shower. When she came downstairs Corin was emerging from the dining room. He shut the door behind him. Then Dad appeared in the hall, wearing his coat.

'I'm off then,' he said, winking at Corin.

'Off where?' asked Holly.

'I've got a date with my best girl. See you later.'

'Where are they going?' Holly turned to Corin in bewilderment.

'Come with me.' Corin opened the dining room door with a flourish and ushered her inside.

The room was in soft candlelight and there was a table set for two.

'Dinner is served — or it will be in a moment,' Corin said. He tilted her chin up so that he could kiss her. 'Happy Valentine's Day, Mrs Grainger.'

11

Tom sat in the office wrestling with the accounts and wondering, not for the first time, if they'd bitten off more than they could chew.

He'd had a notice put on the hotel's website that it would be re-opening under new management at the end of March, and bookings were starting to come in for April onwards. Holly had a bookings spreadsheet on her laptop and would transfer the information to their new computer system when it was installed.

A website for the hotel had been set up by a nephew of Charlie Mack's some time ago. Presumably he had intended that Charlie would then look after it. It now looked out of date. Tom had been in touch with the nephew to make small changes, but it needed a major upgrade with, of course, the new name. More money going out. And the sign proclaiming the Bridge Inn, with 'formerly the Ferryboat' underneath, would be delivered next week — that had been more expensive to make than Tom had anticipated.

But the weather forecasters were saying it was going to be a hot summer. If they were right, that would be good for business. The area was popular with hill walkers and hopefully some sunshine would bring them out in droves. Corin's cooking would attract gourmet customers, and he and Judy were working on plans for meals that would appeal to families with children too. There was a piece of garden at the side of the hotel that would be a great site for a children's play area.

They might be short of money but they weren't short of ideas.

Tom flicked through a pile of brochures and leaflets Corin had picked up the last time he was in Oban. Some of the local attractions were closed over the winter — the castles and stately homes and gardens. But there were all-year-round sporting activities, with companies organising such things as wildlife safaris and kayaking expeditions, and of course there was the new golf course opening soon. He must start now to ask these companies if they could work together to set up special packages for visitors. Apart from Januaries, when they would close the hotel and take their own holiday, they would have to work really hard to attract customers every month of the year. It was all so different from running the B&B where nearby Luton airport ensured a houseful of customers all year round.

He reached for the laptop and found the hotel website. There was the lovely review Miss Fisher had posted. And she'd promised to come back later in the year.

The banner heading, along with a picture of the hotel, showed the current ferryboat, one of many that had ploughed the waters between Lorn and

North Lorn for hundreds of years. Tom was suddenly assailed by doubt. Had he been too hasty in changing the name of the hotel? Rewriting history too quickly, maybe? What had Garry meant by saying 'You can try'?

His head seemed too full of questions to which he couldn't see the answers. A walk sometimes helped when he felt like that, especially here where the grandeur of the hills and the movement of the water, not to mention the neighbours stopping to say hello, distracted him from his problems.

He shut the computer down and went upstairs, where Judy was engaged in sorting out the linen cupboard. 'Are you free for a walk for twenty minutes?' he asked her.

Judy stopped counting sheets. 'Oh, yes. Just what I could do with.' She made a note on a piece of paper. 'Some of these sheets will need replacing very soon. I'll get my jacket.'

She tucked her hand through Tom's arm as they made their way out of the hotel grounds. 'Mum phoned,' she said.

'Everything going all right?' Tom asked.

'Swimmingly,' said Judy. 'Doesn't sound as if Louise is missing us at all! Mum had some friends from her art evening class round last night. Louise gave them all manicures and they helped with her homework — pop artists in the 1960s!'

Tom laughed. 'Did Marilyn mention Eddie?'

'Mention Eddie! She hardly stopped talking about him. He's round there every day. Mum's practically adopted him, from the sound of things.'

'He's a — ' began Tom.

'Nice boy,' Judy finished his sentence. 'I know, he is. But they're out at parties and clubs all the time, not just at weekends. Is love's young dream distracting Louise too much from her schoolwork? That's what I would like to know.'

12

Angus was at school. Lizzie was at work. The cottage was as clean and tidy as it was possible to be when there was a five-year-old boy around. There was nothing to do in the garden.

Iris stared out of the window wondering how to fill the rest of her day. She could sit and read a book of course, or knit the jumper with a dinosaur on the front she was making for Angus. But she wanted a job. She needed a job. The notice she'd put in the shop window hadn't brought any responses.

How would her life have been if Fin hadn't roared into it that summer? She'd abandoned her ambition to study music to marry him. And she'd abandoned Sandy Mack and their budding relationship without a second thought. She'd been so in love. So young. The window blurred in front of her.

Roberta walked past, back from her morning walk to collect her newspaper from the post office-cum-shop a mile away. Iris wiped her eyes and rapped on the glass, then beckoned a startled Roberta to come in.

'What's up?' she asked as she took off her coat.

'Nothing. That's the problem,' Iris said.

Roberta knew just what Iris meant. Plus, she might be retired, but she was still a teacher. 'Get some paper and a pen,' she commanded. 'OK. Let's make a list of possibilities.' She stopped. 'Actually, let's not. I've just had a brainwave.'

'What?' asked Iris, amused in spite of her gloomy mood. Roberta could always be guaranteed to cheer her up.

'You make a lovely fruit cake. And a good cup of tea.'

'Ye-es.' Iris couldn't see where this was leading.

'It's a pity I didn't think of this before, and of course the ferry won't be around for much longer. On the other hand, with the weather being chilly, people will be more likely to appreciate it.' Roberta beamed at Iris. 'Don't you think that's a good idea?'

'What?' Iris said again. 'What's a good idea?'

'Sell cake and a hot drink to folk in the ferry queue, of course. It won't make you a fortune but it would be much appreciated.'

Iris considered. In the summer the queues for the ferry could stretch back for half a mile. It was one of the reasons why the bridge was being built. In the winter, though, you didn't have to wait very long to get on the four-car ferryboat. But Roberta's plan was worth thinking about if only to get her out of the house. She tried to think it through.

'But how would it work — would I have to get loads of flasks or what?'

Roberta jumped up. 'You know that

tall chap? I think he's in charge of the bridge workers. We'll go and ask him if we can use an electricity socket in that hut they've got to boil a kettle.'

Before she knew it Iris was being whisked out of her front door and down the piece of new road that led to the bridge. The 'tall chap' was there, poring over some drawings. Iris let Roberta do the talking.

'Well,' he said when Roberta had succinctly outlined her plan, 'I'll think about it. Can you come back tomorrow?' He grinned. 'As long as there's a nice slice of cake in it for me — yes, what is it?'

A man with a large fluffy moustache stood in the doorway. 'Boss, there's something you need to see.'

The boss sighed and folded up his papers. 'Not more trouble, I hope.'

'I'm afraid so.' Fluffy Moustache stood aside in an elaborately polite gesture to let Roberta and Iris past.

As they walked away Iris heard the boss say something about CCTV. So, the rumours about vandalism on the bridge must be true. Who would want to do that?

Iris felt despondent again as she said goodbye to Roberta. The plan seemed futile in the cold light of day. Even if every driver and passenger bought a snack from her she would make hardly anything, not after she'd bought all the ingredients. And wouldn't she have to get a permit or something?

'Hello. It's Iris, isn't it?' Holly Grainger had stopped her car and wound down the window. Iris went over and crouched down to talk to her.

'How are you settling in?'

'It's a learning curve,' Holly laughed. 'I've just been along to the little shop. It's an Aladdin's cave, isn't it?' Her face became more serious. 'I — I saw your notice in the shop window. Dad says we'll probably need some help when the season kicks in.'

'Thanks,' Iris said. Meaning, thanks for nothing.

'Would you like to come in and have

a coffee?' Holly asked impulsively. 'I love it here but I miss my friends in Glasgow. They're all waiting until the hotel is properly opened before they come up.'

Why not, Iris thought. It wasn't as if she had anything else to do.

Sitting at the so-familiar kitchen table in the Ferryboat she felt she'd been churlish, as Holly made a cafetiere of coffee and poured it into a couple of pretty cups, chatting all the while. She made an effort to sound upbeat.

'The place is looking better already,' she said. 'I love the wallpaper you used in the hall. It makes a really good first impression.'

Holly sat down. 'It was fun planning it all. Mum and Dad were great; they gave me a free hand with the colours and everything. If I wasn't in the hotel business I'd be an interior designer. The bedrooms are nearly finished — I'll show you if you like. Oh! Iris, you might be able to help.'

Iris put down her cup. 'How?'

'We can't find that big blue book that Mr Mack used for bookings. He wouldn't have taken it with him accidentally, would he?'

'I can ask him if you like,' Iris said. 'Everything was in such a muddle his last few days here. Have you tried his room?'

'The office?'

'No, the wee room next to it. He used it as a bedroom and sitting-room for himself. Shall we have a look?'

The room wasn't one that would be in the public domain, so it was presently being used as a repository for unpacked boxes and furniture that had yet to find a home. There were shelves under the window with a curtain across them. In with a jumble of old travel guides and local history titles was the blue book.

Holly opened it. 'Can you read his writing?' she asked, handing it over.

Iris scanned the page and then looked at Holly, her eyes wide. 'He's got a party of four booked in for dinner, bed and breakfast tomorrow night.'

13

It had been a hectic thirty-six hours, installing the new beds, hanging curtains, getting the electrician to make last-minute adjustments to the lighting, and a host of other things to get the rooms ready for paying guests. Then there were the finishing touches — the tea-trays with their tins of homemade shortbread, the locally sourced toiletries, the folders of tourist information. But it had been worth it. The guests, two couples on their way to a wedding followed by a week's holiday on the Isle of Skye, had professed themselves so pleased with the accommodation and their dinner and breakfast that they'd arranged to stay a night on their way back south.

It was a good start, thought Holly as she changed the bed in the room with the lovely view of the loch. And well deserved, though she said so herself! Even though the spring sunshine was only feebly filtering its way through the clouds this morning, the room looked warm and golden, exactly how she had envisaged it.

The bedroom next door had been equally appreciated. And of course the visitors had raved over Corin's dinner. Well, three of them had. One of the men seemed harder to please, taking a long time to choose what he wanted to eat and bemoaning the absence of his favourite vintage from the wine list.

When she went downstairs to the kitchen she found Judy frowning over a text message. 'Louise wants to go to Italy with Eddie and his family over Easter. 'Hope you don't mind,' she says, when we haven't seen her for weeks! Right. I'll be on the phone the minute she comes home from school. This isn't something to sort out by texting. And what about Granmar? It's very selfish of Louise to expect her to travel up here on her own.'

'I'm sure Granmar will cope. She drives all over the place,' Holly said. She refused Judy's offer of coffee and poured herself a glass of water. She hadn't enjoyed her breakfast coffee; the new brand they'd ordered seemed to her to have a metallic taste. She must speak to Corin about it. 'But, Mum, we're getting bookings now for the Easter holidays. I'm not sure where we'll all sleep.'

'I thought we'd get Mr Mack's old bedroom through there cleared out and put a sofa bed in it for your father and me. Then Granmar and Louise, if she comes, can share our room in the annexe.'

Holly nodded. 'Good idea.' The chaotic little room, where the book-in book had eventually been run to earth thanks to Iris, was one they'd shut the door on so far. For a moment she remembered with longing the high-ceilinged Victorian rooms of the flat she and Corin had lived in, in Glasgow. Their first married home. The sitting-room with its sanded floors and big bay window. The bedroom from where they could see the winter moon through the trees in the park. All that space, just for them. If only they could transport that flat here to give them privacy, a place to call their own.

Then she shook herself. This hotel was what Corin wanted, and Mum and Dad had been heroes, the way they'd been willing to relocate and work so hard to make it a real family business. She wasn't going to be the one to let the side down.

'I've finished upstairs,' she said. 'I'll make a start now on that room, shall I? I hope we've got plenty of bin bags. I don't think it's been tidied since the year dot.'

★   ★   ★

'Louise?' Judy pressed the speaker on her phone so that Tom and Holly could hear the conversation from both ends.

'Mum. Hi! What's up?'

'Nothing's up. Just wanted to speak to you, darling. Your dad and I were looking forward to seeing you at Easter, so . . .'

'I so was, too — looking forward to seeing you, I mean. But Ed's family are going to Rome and asked me if I'd like to go and the architecture is really cool there. I've always wanted to see it.'

Judy raised her eyebrows at her husband and elder daughter as Louise waxed lyrical on the beauty of Rome's ancient buildings.

'So, you're saying it would be an educational trip?' she asked when she got a word in edgewise.

Her light sarcasm was lost on Louise. 'Totally. Thanks, Mum!'

Judy shrugged helplessly. 'You seem to have it all settled. Can I speak to Granmar?'

'She's getting her roots done. She'll be back in an hour or so.'

'I'll call her later. Did it occur to you, Louise, that Granmar would appreciate company when she comes up here? It's a very long drive from Harpenden.'

'Oh, Granmar's not planning to go at Easter either,' Louise said blithely. 'Ages ago, long before you moved, she booked a painting holiday in Devon.'

'I see.' Judy pursed her lips. 'Well, let's think. If it doesn't interfere with your exams maybe you could come up on the May bank holiday weekend?'

'I'll check my timetable and run that past Eddie,' Louise said.

'I meant . . . ' Judy stopped. 'Of course Eddie will be welcome too. Tell Granmar I'll catch her later. Here's your dad for a quick word, sweetheart.'

She handed the phone to Tom.

Perhaps sensing that Judy was about to expostulate, Tom carried the phone into the hall and took it off the speaker facility. Judy could faintly hear his side of the conversation as he put an amusing slant on their new life and didn't refer to Louise's Easter plans.

'What do you think of that?' Judy flopped into a chair and looked at Holly. 'What are you laughing at?'

Holly came over and squeezed her mother's shoulders. 'You must take after your father,' she said. 'Granmar's free artistic spirit skipped a generation! Louise does miss us, Mum, of course she does. And she really wants to see us and the hotel, but this opportunity's come to go somewhere she's dreamed of and her head's in the clouds.'

Judy smiled reluctantly. 'You're right. I've known my mother for almost fifty years and she still surprises me. I expect I'll say the same about Louise when she's middle-aged.'

14

'How's life at the 'boat?' Roberta hailed Tom as he passed her garden during the daily fifteen-minute constitutional he allowed himself. His walks frequently took him down to the pier and the company of Donnie. He enjoyed Donnie's yarns about the area — while suspecting some of them to be tall tales — and his amusingly forthright opinions on the demise of ferries. Having found out that Donnie played the piano accordion, he'd engaged him to play in the hotel one night a week, and that was proving popular with the regulars.

So he was intrigued by this woman to whom his new friend had apparently been engaged for — how many years was it? Not, of course, that he'd discussed that particular subject with Donnie . . . but he'd heard Judy and Holly speculating about it.

It's called the Bridge Inn now, said Tom, but only to himself. His qualms over the name change had morphed into a certainty that he'd done the wrong thing. It seemed that to Roberta, and every one of the locals, the hotel would always be the Ferryboat, the 'boat for short.

'Going well,' he said aloud. 'Four booked in for dinner, bed and breakfast tonight.' He leaned on the gate. 'Your garden's looking good. What have you planted?'

Roberta looked around with dissatisfaction. 'I'd love a bigger plot. I've put in beetroot and spring onions here today, and marigolds there. Come in — I've got a small greenhouse round the back. I'll show you.'

Tom admired the neat shelves of pots with plants at various stages of growth. 'Your fingers are very green!' he said. 'Corin and I have been talking about having a kitchen garden. Perhaps you could tell us what grows best in this part of the world and what won't work?'

Roberta's eyes lit up. 'I certainly could. Shall I come up this afternoon?'

'Er, OK. That would be great.' Tom was taken aback by her immediate enthusiasm. 'There is a vegetable garden but it's all overgrown. It'll be a lot of work.'

'The sooner we get started the better, if you want veggies this year.'

Tom grinned, nodding his thanks. Roberta didn't hang around. His eyes fell on two wooden half-barrels. 'We're getting a couple of these for the front entrance. I'm sure I remember there being some but they've gone.'

He was surprised to see Roberta look discomfited. 'Confession time, Tom. These are the same tubs. Iris was trying to jazz up the hotel before potential buyers saw it. We took these up when the fuchsias were in bloom.'

'That explains it,' Tom burst out laughing. 'Judy and I thought we had a tub burglar on our hands at the — at the Bridge Inn.'

'It was Iris's idea,' Roberta said

again. 'And it worked, didn't it?' She led the way out of the greenhouse and wiped her muddy hands on her skirt. 'Tom, if I may speak frankly . . . The 'Bridge Inn' — what's that all about?'

Tom groaned. 'It seemed a good idea at the time. New owners, new bridge. I rushed into it.'

'If you take my advice you'll rush out of it. The bridge will bring changes, you're right, but the 'boat will always be the 'boat. I'll see you later.' The latch of her gate gave a loud click as she shut it behind him.

'If I may speak frankly', Roberta had said. That was the only way she ever spoke, as far as Tom could make out. He quailed at the consequences of not taking her advice, of getting off to a bad start with the locals — and quailed too at the thought of how much the new sign had cost. What was he to do?

His dilemma went completely from his mind as he opened the front door.

'Dad!' Holly was running downstairs. 'Something awful's happened. There's water coming down into the yellow bedroom. The back wall is dripping wet.'

'Have you phoned a plumber?' Holly nodded. 'And the dining room? Has the water reached the ground floor?'

'I don't know. Corin's crawling around the attic to see where it's come from.'

'It'll be the water tank. Did any of you turn the water off at the main?' Holly lifted her shoulders in reply. Tom threw off his jacket. 'Where's your mother?'

'Laying out every pan and bucket we have underneath the water. But we've got those people coming back tonight.'

And only one bedroom available now. Tom hurried through to the hall cupboard to find the water main and then to the kitchen to run the taps. Why had Corin not thought to do that?

★　★　★

The water had slowed to a trickle before the plumber arrived. Fortunately

90

the damage seemed to have been confined to the bedroom. Tom checked the dining room ceiling at close quarters and found it bore no evidence of damp. While he was there he ran his fingers over a strange little circle. As far as he could remember it corresponded with one of similar size in the bedroom floor above, as if a hole had been filled in. Odd.

'Sorry, Tom,' Corin said contritely from the bottom of the ladder. 'I didn't have a clue what to do.'

'Your father never showed you what a water main looks like?'

'Dad wouldn't know a water main if it bit him in the leg.' Corin grinned up at him. 'Mum's the practical one. She does all the DIY stuff.'

Despite his anxieties, Tom couldn't help feeling a rush of pleasure at the news. Here was something Mr Big Cheese Solicitor couldn't do!

'I think I'm more like Dad than Mum in that respect,' Corin added.

'Nonsense, son,' said Tom, climbing

down. 'It's easy when you know how. I can show you . . . '

'Dad . . . ' Holly stuck an anxious face round the door. 'Can you come? The guests have arrived. And one of them's not too pleased. He's insisting on speaking to you.'

Once Tom had got the water under control he'd phoned the hotel nearest them, about three miles away, and asked if they could accommodate two of his guests. It seemed to be the only solution.

But the man who'd been the grumpy one of the party a week earlier was having none of it.

'We want two rooms together, as booked,' he maintained. 'It's your problem. Sort it out. At your expense.'

His wife looked apologetically at Tom.

'I'm sorry about your flood,' she said. 'I do hope we can have dinner here as planned though. We've been telling everyone we know about the meal we had last week.'

'Of course,' said Tom. 'And I'll call and reserve another room for you, sir.'

As he reached for the phone he could see Roberta as she stopped to look at the Bridge Inn board. She shook her head before making her determined way down the front path.

He smiled at the man through gritted teeth.

What with the flood and its consequences, and the apparently inevitable purchase of another new hotel sign, it was proving to be a very expensive day.

15

Iris folded the ironing board and put it away. Another morning spent on tasks she could have finished in half the time but eked out because she had nothing else to fill the hours before Angus came home from school.

She had considered Roberta's idea of selling hot drinks and cakes to ferry travellers, but it wasn't a practical proposition. It might have been a sound plan with summer's long queues. But one big stumbling block was the use of the power point for a kettle in the workman's hut. While the tall foreman had seemed accommodating, it was his deputy, the man Iris thought of as Fluffy Moustache, who had been there on his own the next time she went down and he'd told her in no uncertain terms that she would be in the way.

The doorbell rang. It wouldn't be

Roberta — she just walked straight in. Too early for the postman.

The silhouette on the other side of the frosted glass looked kind of familiar. As she came nearer to the door her heart suddenly felt as fractured as the view in front of her.

Sandy Mack. She had time to take a deep breath before she opened the door.

Same tousled fair hair, was her first thought. Broader in the shoulders was her second. Her third thought got lost as she found herself enveloped in a brotherly hug.

'Iris. You haven't changed a bit.'

That wasn't true but it was nice of him to say it.

'Did you ... I wrote ... Your uncle ... ' The words tumbled out, the sentences remaining unfinished.

Sandy was part of that summer six years ago when Fin's motorbike had roared off the ferry and into her life. She hadn't seen him since the day she told him that she was getting on that bike and leaving Lorn, leaving him and their blossoming romance. Seeing him brought it all back — the whirlwind relationship with Fin, and its ending.

'Are you going to ask me in?' His voice was teasing but kind.

'Of course.' Iris opened the door wider.

'I only got your letter last week,' Sandy said, ducking his head through the living-room door. 'I'd left that company and it was a while before it caught up with me. I've got another contract but it hasn't started yet so I've come home. Thanks for being concerned about Uncle Charlie. How is he?'

'You haven't seen him?'

'Flew into Glasgow this morning, hired a car and came straight here.'

'I'm worried about him. I've called on him a couple of time since he moved but he's chatted on the doorstep, never said come in for a coffee or anything. Not like him. I don't think he's looking after himself.'

'Do you want to walk up there with me now?' asked Sandy. 'Give him a surprise?'

Iris nodded. 'Surely he'll ask *you* in,' she said, going for her jacket.

'How are things with yourself, Iris?' asked Sandy as they went through Lorn and up the hill road to Charlie's. 'I was really sorry to hear about . . . you know. So you and Lizzie are living in your aunt's cottage. How's that working out?' He looked at her quizzically.

Iris laughed. 'You remember Lizzie, then? But no, she's been great, the proverbial tower of strength. We couldn't have done without her at the beginning, Angus and I. But now I worry that we're holding her back.'

'How do you mean?'

'She hates her job in the bank but I think she feels she can't make a change because it would affect us as well. She gave up her flat-share in Oban to come . . . after it happened . . . but what she's always wanted to do is move to Glasgow and work in a department store. And really Angus and I would be fine now on our own.'

Sandy stopped to look at her as they turned in at Charlie's gate.

'And what's it like being a mum? Sounds very grown-up.'

'It certainly makes you grow up fast,' Iris said. She bent down to pluck a weed from the gravel path. 'Do you want to come and eat with us one night? Then you can meet Angus.'

Sandy rang the bell. 'I'd like to do that. I'm planning to be here for a while if Charlie will have me.'

'I hear him coming now,' Iris said.

Charlie's voice sounded quavery as he held out his hand to his nephew. 'Good to see you, Sandy. Good to see you.' He paused uncertainly.

Sandy glanced at Iris and in one smooth movement, giving Charlie no time to prevent them, they stepped one on either side of him into the house.

Charlie followed them into the kitchen and stood with his head bent like a schoolboy waiting to be told off.

Iris took charge. 'You two sit down,' she said. 'I'll put the kettle on, shall I?'

The problem would be finding clean mugs, clean anything really. Had Charlie really done no washing-up since he'd moved in? That's what it looked like. At least there was hot water in the tap. She filled the sink, washed three mugs and put a pile of other dishes in to soak.

The fridge held fresh milk and not much else.

'No biscuits, sorry,' said Charlie.

'Never mind biscuits,' said Iris. 'You'll make yourself ill, Charlie, if you don't eat properly.'

Sandy leaned forward. 'I was never going to take it over, you know,' he said. 'I wish I — '

'I know,' said Charlie. 'It's a pity, but there you go. You're a credit to the family, Sandy. A clever lad. And I think the old 'boat is in good hands, from what I've heard. It's just . . . after all these years living with other people around I can't get used to being on my own.' He lifted his coffee with a shaky hand. 'How long are you here for?'

'I've got a few weeks before I need to go back to Switzerland,' Sandy said.

Charlie's eyes lit up. 'You'll stay here? I'll make up a bed for you.'

'I'll do it,' said Sandy. 'You sit there, Uncle Charlie. The place needs a bit of straightening up, I think you'll agree. You'll feel better when it's clean and tidy.'

'I'll make a start, shall I?' Iris said. 'Sandy, why don't you get your car and take Charlie to do some food shopping? Good healthy stuff, mind.'

When they'd gone she found Charlie's radio and turned on the classical music channel. Then she rolled up her sleeves and looked around, smiling ruefully at herself in the dusty mirror.

It didn't look as if she'd have any problem filling the rest of her day.

16

Judy left the large squashy parcel until last, recognising Marilyn's handwriting. Her mother never gave up trying to get Judy out of her favourite jeans and check overshirts. What would it be for this year's birthday?

'Mum, that's lovely!' Holly exclaimed as Judy held up a floaty top in a shade somewhere between blue and purple. 'You'll look great in that colour.'

Judy thought of the drawerful of pretty things her mother had given her over the years, most of which she'd never worn. 'Why can't she choose something more practical?' she asked, feeling guilty as she spoke.

'Because,' said Holly, 'that's all you ever choose for yourself.'

Judy had to acknowledge the truth of this. 'But it's such a waste,' she said. 'I can't even pass them on to you as we're different shapes.'

'Why should they go to waste?' Holly asked. 'Wear that one tonight. Corin's going to make a special dinner for you, early, before the customers arrive. I'll be your waitress for the evening!'

'But . . .' Wearing the top wasn't just a matter of pulling it over her head. She'd have to find her smartest pair of trousers to go underneath it, and the length of them dictated digging out her one pair of high heels. And what would her usual face be like, above such glamour — no make-up and easy-to-care-for hair? She would look ridiculous. 'You know I hate getting dressed up.'

'We'll have a makeover session, if we have time,' promised Holly. 'And I've got some earrings that would look perfect with it.'

Judy smiled at her, thinking how lovely it was living with her even-tempered elder daughter again. Holly's hazel eyes and long lashes were enhanced by immaculate make-up, but to Judy's mind she would look just as gorgeous without any. But she was looking pale and, Judy realised, had not eaten much lunch.

'Are you all right, love?' she asked.

'I'm fine.' Holly jumped up. 'Right, madam — your bedroom, five thirty? You bring yourself. I will bring my make-up bag and straighteners. Prepare to be amazed,' she said to Tom as he came into the kitchen.

'Amazed about what?' Tom asked but Holly left the room laughing, declining to enlighten him. He held his hands out, asking Judy the same question.

She shook her head. She knew that Tom loved her even if she didn't spend hours fussing over her appearance, but perhaps it would be nice to make an effort occasionally. Especially now, when birthdays seemed to come along with alarming frequency.

'Wait and see.' Judy began to load the dishwasher. 'Tom,' she said over her shoulder, 'do you think Holly's looking a bit peaky?'

'I hadn't noticed,' Tom said. 'Tired,

probably, like the rest of us. Jude, I'm expecting Roberta to come up this afternoon. She might go straight to the garden, but if she rings the bell tell her that's where I am.'

'Will do. Oh, Tom — can you be here in the kitchen by six-ish? Quick birthday dinner. Made specially for us by an up-and-coming young chef.'

'Sounds good.' He gave her a quick kiss. 'See you later, birthday girl.'

Tom didn't know Roberta very well if he thought she would ring the bell to announce herself. Judy was making desserts from Corin's recipes for tonight's guests when she heard, 'Cooee! It's me!', and then Roberta pushed open the kitchen door.

If, Judy found herself thinking, there was a what-not-to-wear competition between Roberta and herself, the judges would have a hard job deciding. Her jeans and check shirt or Roberta's ancient sweater, sturdy skirt and gum-boots? But of course Roberta was dressed for an afternoon's digging.

'Tom's in the garden,' she said. 'He really appreciates your help.'

Roberta came over to the table and peered into the bowl Judy was holding. For a moment Judy thought she was going to stick her finger in for a lick. 'Marmalade ice cream,' she said, laying the bowl on the work surface and changing the subject. 'It's been a great success having Donnie play here on Saturday nights.'

'He and Iris often play at functions together,' Roberta said, an innocent expression on her face.

'Really? What does Iris play?'

'The violin. Very well. Would have studied music if things had turned out otherwise. Gave up her place at college to marry a man she hardly knew. Had a child. Widowed at twenty-three.' She shook her head. 'Men are just trouble.'

'Even Donnie?' Judy asked, laughing.

'Especially Donnie,' Roberta said firmly but with a smile in her voice. 'So that's settled then?'

'What's settled?'

'Iris and Donnie. Playing here. Don't know why old Charlie never thought of it. Great idea, Judy. Right. I'll be off to get my hands dirty.'

Judy turned back to the ice cream. She couldn't recall the exact words of their conversation, but it was clear that Roberta was very clever at getting her own way.

★　★　★

Judy sat in the place of honour at the kitchen table a few hours later while Corin busied himself making something delicious-smelling at the cooker. Holly sat beside her while Tom went to fetch a bottle of sparkling wine.

She looked down at herself. The top was a lovely colour but her hands, with their coat of red nail polish, looked unfamiliar. The weight of Holly's earrings felt odd too. But you had to suffer to be beautiful . . . perhaps Holly would take a photograph of her in all her glory to send to Marilyn.

'Happy birthday, sweetheart.' Tom leant down to kiss her. 'You look very nice. Have you done something to your hair?'

Judy grinned at Holly. 'I've been to the hairdresser,' she said as Tom handed her a glass.

Holly shook her head when it was her turn. 'I don't think I should.' She raised her voice. 'Corin . . . ' she said, and he came over and put his arm round her. 'Mum, Dad, we didn't mean . . . I think I . . . I'm having a baby. I'm sorry.'

'Sorry? It's wonderful news!' Judy got up to hug her daughter. 'A baby. Isn't it lovely, Tom?'

Tom looked quite overcome and covered his emotion with a joke. 'I'm far too young to be a granddad,' he said, shaking Corin's hand.

'Of course we wanted a baby, but we thought it would be a few years yet, when we were more settled here,' Holly said. 'I hope I'll be able to pull my weight.'

'It's lovely,' said Judy again. 'We'll

manage, don't worry. Have you told Philip and Verity yet? Off you go and do that. And I'll phone Granmar and Louise. What an absolutely brilliant birthday present.'

17

'This is parsley and these are chives,' Roberta told Angus. His little fingers were just the right size for potting up the herbs. 'When it's warmer we'll take them out of the greenhouse and put them in the garden. The weathermen say it's going to be a good summer. OK, I think we're finished in here.'

'Dig?' asked Angus hopefully.

'No digging in my garden today. But if you want to come up to the hotel with me there's a lot of digging to do in their garden.'

Today Iris and Lizzie were painting their sitting-room and Roberta had volunteered to take Angus out of their way. It was a pleasure for both of them — getting mucky in 'Robbie's' garden was one of Angus's favourite things to do.

'We're going to two other places

first,' Roberta told Angus, reaching for his hand. 'We're going to see Charlie who used to live in the hotel, remember? And then we'll pop down to see Donnie and have a look round the ferryboat if you like.'

'I do like the ferryboat,' Angus said, smiling up at her.

He looked uncannily like his mother, Roberta thought, with his light brown hair and delicate features. But whereas Iris's eyes were grey, Angus's were blazing blue, an inheritance from his father. Roberta hadn't known Iris very well six years ago; she'd just been aware of her in the background of the hotel that summer. But she remembered the consternation of Iris's great-aunt, with whom she was staying at Brook Cottage, when Iris announced she was leaving with Fin only weeks after they met. And she remembered three years ago when the news came that Fin had not survived an accident on that motorbike of his.

Now Iris's first love, Sandy, was back

in town, as it were, although not for long. Apparently he was much in demand for his IT skills and hired himself out on lucrative short-term contracts. It was hard to believe that the go-getting young man was any relative of Charlie Mack's.

It would be a treat for Charlie to see Angus, Roberta thought now. He'd always made a fuss of the little boy when Iris brought him to the hotel, bringing him crisps and lemonade from the bar and letting him swivel round on his office chair.

Both Charlie and Sandy were in the house. It was very tidy and smelling of furniture polish, so it looked as though Sandy was keeping up Iris's good work.

Charlie installed Angus on a little footstool and went to find him a snack.

'Hey Angus,' said Sandy, 'do you remember that trick I showed you when I came to tea at your house?'

Angus bounced in anticipation. 'The one with the penny?'

'The very one.' Sandy put his hand

behind Angus's head and apparently pulled a ten pence piece from his ear. 'Let's see if there's one on the other side.'

There was. With eyes as big as saucers Angus carefully tucked the coins into his pocket.

Sandy turned to Roberta. 'What will Donnie do when the ferry stops?'

What a nice-looking lad he was, Roberta thought. Not handsome, exactly, but with a friendly, open face.

'Tinker about with engines,' she replied, and was about to elaborate on this when Charlie came through from the kitchen with a chocolate biscuit for Angus.

'And when's Donnie going to get you to the altar?' he asked Roberta, a twinkle in his eye.

'How do you put up with him?' Roberta raised her eyebrows at Sandy. 'To every thing there is a season,' she said loftily to Charlie, who chuckled and nudged her in the ribs with his elbow.

He certainly seemed very cheery today, she thought, when she and Angus walked down to the pier. But how would he be when Sandy went away again?

Angus tugged her hand. 'The boat is in.'

Roberta could see Donnie with one of the bridge workers — the one with the moustache who had been brusque with Iris.

'Shouting,' Angus said as they got closer.

Roberta was torn between finding out what on earth was going on and not wanting Angus to hear anything he shouldn't.

But Donnie was walking towards her, visibly angry. 'This idiot has just accused me of vandalising the bridge!'

Fluffy Moustache took off in the other direction. 'You're the one with something to gain from the delay, Campbell,' he called over his shoulder. 'It's got to be you.'

18

Sandy was showing Tom how to update the website. He'd redesigned it, and the banner proclaiming the Ferryboat showed the newly whitewashed building with Tom and Judy standing smiling at the front door. With their very own tubs of geraniums!

There were new buttons to click to see the bedrooms, sample menus, and links to local attractions — even one for the view from the dining-room window. Tom was thrilled with it and found Sandy to be a patient tutor in all that had to be done behind the scenes.

'Your uncle will miss you when you go back to Switzerland,' he said, having been kept up to date on the subject by Roberta during their gardening sessions.

'I've arranged for Iris to go in a few days a week,' Sandy said. 'Kind of home-help. And Donnie and Roberta will keep an eye on him. He was in a slump, not knowing what to do with himself, but I think he's on the up now.'

'What do you think about this vandalism business?' Tom asked. 'Obviously it's nothing to do with Donnie. But someone's doing it.'

'Has to be one of the bridge workers, I think,' Sandy said. 'Someone who knows how to use those industrial cutting tools. But the foreman told me he suspects the owner of a company who didn't get the painting contract.'

'Too bad that someone — that guy with the big moustache and the short temper — is spreading rumours about Donnie.' Tom shook his head.

'Apart from it being against the law, Donnie wouldn't do anything sneaky like that,' said Sandy. 'I've known him all my life and I've never heard a word against him.'

Tom saw the opportunity to discuss Donnie's love life with someone other than Judy or Holly. 'So what is it with

Donnie and Roberta?' he asked, lowering his voice. 'Have they really been engaged for eleven years? Do you think they'll ever get married?'

'Your guess is as good as mine, Tom — and everyone else's,' Sandy chuckled. 'Donnie can talk the hind leg off a donkey, as you know, and Roberta is hardly discreet as a rule, but on that topic they are both absolutely mum.'

'Maybe they are secretly married,' Tom surmised, 'and laughing up their sleeves at us.'

'I thought you were learning how to look after the website, Tom Jeffrey. And they say women are gossips!' Judy stood in the doorway. 'I'm sorry to drag you away but the downstairs loo is blocked again.'

Sandy pressed a few keys on the computer and the beautiful new website with the loch view and the geranium tubs disappeared. 'It's all glamour in the hotel business!' he said. 'I'll leave you to it, Tom. You know where I am if you need me, but I think you've got the hang of it.'

'It was a learning curve,' Tom said. 'New tricks, old dogs.' He held out his hand to Sandy. 'See you again soon, I hope; and let us know if there's anything we can do to help with Charlie.'

'There is, actually. Well, not help exactly, but I thought as this is my last night I'd take him and Iris here for dinner, if you've got a table for three?'

'No problem,' Judy said. 'Come and I'll put your name in the book. What time would suit you?'

Tom was just about to go and get to grips with the plumbing problem when the phone rang. He could see from the new call display unit that it was Philip and debated with himself whether to answer it or not. It was ridiculous. He was going to be fifty this year but Philip made him feel like a callow youth.

Philip's visit with his Edinburgh golfing friends earlier in the month had been very successful. The newly opened course was pronounced to be 'a blinder' and they went home with plans to return at the earliest opportunity. Perhaps he was phoning now to make the booking, although that call should be made to the front desk number not their own line. But Philip wouldn't make that distinction. These thoughts shot through Tom's mind as he dithered with his hand above the phone. Then he took a deep breath and lifted the receiver. It wouldn't look good from Philip's end, hearing the phone ringing and nobody answering.

'Philip! Good to hear from you.' Tom cleared his throat. 'How is Verity?'

'Well, very well. And how is our future grandchild progressing?'

'Holly's fine,' Tom said. When Philip had heard the news about the baby he'd said to Tom that they would have to have a chat about 'making financial provision' for it. Tom hoped he wasn't wanting to have that chat now.

But Philip had other things on his mind. 'Splendid. Now, I'm waiting for

118

the chaps to let me know what dates they're free to come back. Wives to consult! But maybe they could come too. If you could find something for our good ladies to do while we're on the golf course that would solve the problem. And double your — our — income.'

'That sounds like an excellent idea.' It did actually, Tom thought, annoyed that he hadn't come up with it. 'Judy and I will see what we can do.'

'Don't take too long about it!' Philip harrumphed. 'We want to get back on that green. Maybe this time you'll be able to join us for a round, Tom?'

Pip is short for Philip, Tom thought. *I shall think of him as Pip. Pip, Pip.*

'Maybe, Pi — Philip. A lot to do here, though. Difficult to get away.' It wasn't the first time Philip had suggested they play together but Tom had always managed to avoid it. Philip was too competitive by half.

'Look, I'll talk to Judy and the others about what you suggest,' he said. 'I'm going to have to go now, Philip. There's something Judy's asked me to do urgently.'

'Good for Judy. Keep you at it! Speak soon.' There was a crash at the other end of the line as Philip replaced the receiver.

'Judy,' Tom called as he went to find his toolbox, 'come and hear what Pip's latest is.'

Judy frowned at him as she came into the hall. 'Don't call him that in Corin's hearing,' she said. 'What does he want now?'

19

Roberta eased herself off her kneeling mat — not a fancy bought one, just a pile of newspapers inside a plastic carrier bag. *My knees are getting creaky in their old age,* she thought. *But a good job done this afternoon, the dahlia bulbs planted.* She loved to see their colourful pom-pom heads in the late summer.

As she leaned over to pick up the mat she caught a glint beside where she'd been working. But it was only a shard of broken glass. She threw it back. Every so often there would be something tantalisingly shiny in the soil and she would hope that, this time, it would be her lost engagement ring.

The ring, a large emerald flanked by two diamonds, had belonged to Donnie's late mother. Roberta had been very fond of her so when Donnie first proposed all those years ago and asked if she'd like that ring or a new one she had no hesitation — what was the point of buying a new one?

Donnie was delighted and liked to see her wearing it. She should have taken it to the jeweller's to get it altered to fit — it was on the large side; her fingers were slimmer in those days — but she kept putting it off. She'd only had it a matter of weeks when she came in from the garden one day and realised it wasn't on her finger.

She wasn't really a jewellery person, but of course the ring was more than that; it was a symbol of Donnie's feelings for her. And it was a Campbell family heirloom. She thought that its loss had got their engagement off to a bad start, although Donnie was philosophical, saying it would turn up eventually. He'd offered to buy her another ring but she refused to let him.

Eleven years of digging in the garden had passed but the earth had declined to give up its secrets.

'Robbie!' At the garden gate Angus was holding up a large brightly coloured box. 'See what Sandy gave me.'

'He was desperate to show you,' Iris said. 'We can come back if it's a bad time.'

'It's a very good time. In you go. I'll wash my hands and put the kettle on.'

When she went into the sitting-room with the tea-tray Angus opened the box and laid out two egg-cups, a little ball and a handkerchief-sized piece of cloth.

'It's a magic set,' he said, his blue eyes sparkling with excitement. 'Robbie, I can make the wee ball disappear. Sandy showed me how.'

'Goodness me.' Roberta put the tray on the table and sat down on the floor beside him. 'I must see this, Mr Magic.'

As Angus arranged his trick Roberta looked up at Iris. Sandy's visit had cheered her up and was also to provide her with some employment, keeping Charlie's house clean and himself fed properly once Sandy was no longer there. But their relationship wasn't just about that, of course; they seemed to get on well together and Roberta knew they'd been an item before that Fin came on the scene. Yesterday afternoon when she'd bumped into Iris in the street Iris had said that Sandy had asked her to have dinner with him at the 'boat that evening.

Roberta's mind didn't usually dwell on romance, her own or anyone else's. Maybe it was because she was thinking of the missing engagement ring (if only Angus had a magic wand to conjure it up) that it occurred to her that perhaps love might have been in the air last night. Iris was young and pretty. It was time she moved on, as they said nowadays. It was a delicate subject, though; maybe she shouldn't bring it up.

'How was your dinner with Sandy?' she asked, tentatively for her. 'Moonlight and roses . . . ?' She held her breath in case Iris was upset at the suggestion.

But Iris shook her head, smiling. 'Sandy's my pal, that's all,' she said. 'He makes me laugh, always has done. It's been great to see him again.' She picked up a biscuit from the tray. 'It was dinner for three last night. Sandy, me and Charlie. It was really weird being in the dining room at the 'boat and not being the waitress. Even weirder for Charlie of course. Mmm — the food was gorgeous. You and Donnie must go.'

'Donnie's not keen on sauces and suchlike. Food messed about as he sees it,' Roberta said.

'He'd like Corin's cooking, I promise,' said Iris. 'The puddings were to die for. I had this lemon and white chocolate . . . OK, all ready, Angus?'

Angus had stood up, his shoulders very straight. 'Ladies and gentlemen,' he said, 'here is my trick.' He bowed and sat down again.

Roberta was genuinely amazed when she pointed at the egg-cup she was sure the ball was in and saw that it was empty when Angus triumphantly whisked off the cloth. She clapped her hands loudly.

Angus tucked his props back into the box. 'There are five more tricks but I don't know how to work them yet.'

'I want to see them when you do.' Roberta felt a rush of love for the little boy. Seeing far too much of children when she was a teacher she'd never wanted to have her own, but being able to borrow Angus occasionally was a great pleasure.

'Has Sandy gone?' she asked Iris as she got up from the floor.

It was Angus who answered, spreading out his arms wide. 'He's flown away. Can we go in an aeroplane, Mummy?' He ran round the room. 'I'm flying to see Sandy in my aeroplane.'

Clearly, Sandy had been a big hit. It would be nice for Angus to have a father, and who would be better than his mother's very good friend?

Roberta bit her tongue hard. She'd said enough on the subject for today.

20

Judy stepped outside the back door. If there had been a shining moon in the sky she would have howled at it, but at six o' clock it was barely visible.

Their much-delayed opening party was happening in an hour's time and there was still such a lot to do. Verity and Iris had been roped in to help Corin with the food preparation but they weren't anywhere near finished. Tom was tearing his hair out because a promised wine delivery hadn't arrived. Holly was feeling peaky but refused to go and lie down. Philip was striding around looking busy but not actually doing anything. There were the extra glasses to wash; flowers to arrange in reception.

And Judy had just got a text from Louise: *Surprise! Didn't want to miss the party. We're two miles away. See you soon!*

The May bank holiday had come and gone. Louise and Eddie had exams the following week, so a visit north was out of the question. Now, a fortnight later, although of course Marilyn and Louise knew about the party, the possibility of them being able to come hadn't arisen. School hadn't broken up and the party was on a Thursday night. But here they were — did 'we' mean Eddie as well? — arriving any minute and nowhere for them to sleep. Why on earth hadn't they let her know earlier?

'Judy, are you OK?'

Judy handed her phone to Tom. 'Surprise, surprise.'

'Good grief,' said Tom, reading the text. 'Well, that's great, isn't it? The family together after all these months.'

'Of course,' Judy said, 'it's wonderful. But — '

'I know. That's your mother and daughter for you. We'll have to go with the flow.'

'All the bedrooms are taken.' Judy

tried to think but her brain seemed to be stuck.

'We'll work something out. Are you coming back in? Verity's persuaded Holly to go to bed for a couple of hours. It's all hands on deck in the kitchen. Thank goodness Holly thought to ask Iris to give us some time this afternoon.'

Judy nodded. 'She's a really hard worker.' As they turned to go inside a large van rumbled into the back yard.

Tom heaved a sigh of relief. 'That's my delivery for the bar.'

Behind the lorry came a car. Louise rolled down the passenger window and waved frantically. 'Mum! Dad! We're here!'

*   *   *

Marilyn joined the food production line in the kitchen. Her quick, coral-tipped fingers spooned fillings into Corin's boat-shaped pastry cases as she told them about the flight to Glasgow and the journey in the hired car up the winding road to Lorn.

Like an excited puppy, Louise ran around the hotel investigating her family's new home. 'Wow!' she exclaimed, looking out of the window at the bridge nearing completion across the loch. 'I must send Eddie a picture. He loves bridges. Will it be finished when we come up in the summer?'

'I don't think so,' Judy said. 'They keep putting the date back.' She put her arms around Louise. 'It's lovely to have you here. But shouldn't you be at school?'

'Nah, I'm on study leave to finish my final art project. Poor old Ed's behind with his so his mum wouldn't let him come up. Can me and Granmar stay until Sunday? We've got a flight booked for Sunday afternoon.'

'Of course,' said Judy, crossing her fingers behind Louise's back. 'Why don't you go over to the annexe and see Holly now?'

'Is she all right?' asked Louise. 'Imagine — me, an auntie!'

'She gets tired easily,' said Judy. 'It's still early days, so I am a little worried about her. She's going to have a scan in a couple of weeks. Can you help this evening, handing food round?'

''Course,' said Louise. 'I'll see Holls, then get changed. Which room am I in?'

'Um, I'll show you later. Look, the annexe is out the front door here and round to the side. Knock gently on the door first.' Judy watched Louise disappear round the corner on her left just as Roberta appeared from the right, her arms full of Michaelmas daisies and marigolds.

'My contribution to the festivities. Where would you like them?'

'They're glorious! Thank you. I wanted to have flowers on the reception desk but I'm running out of time.'

'Get me something to stick them in and I'll do it,' offered Roberta. 'How's it going for the big do?' she asked as she followed Judy to a cupboard in the hall from which Judy produced a green glass vase. 'All set?'

'Almost there,' said Judy. 'Can I leave you to it, Roberta? I need to sort out sleeping arrangements. My mother and younger daughter have turned up unexpectedly.' She tried not to let her thoughts show in her face as Roberta roughly stripped the stems of their leaves and crammed the pretty flowers into the vase without attempting to make any kind of arrangement.

'There, all done,' said Roberta, wiping one hand against the other. 'Look, I imagine the hotel's full to the gunnels tonight. I've got a spare room if that's any use to you.'

Judy could have kissed her. 'Really? Well, if you wouldn't mind your house being an extension of the hotel, that would be brilliant. A business arrangement, of course. Come through and meet my mum.'

She led Roberta through to the kitchen, made the introductions and left the two ladies to get to know each other. Out of the kitchen window she could see Tom and the van driver struggling with boxes of wine bottles. Why couldn't Philip go and help instead of picking at the canapés and getting in everyone's way?

He caught her eye and called across the kitchen. 'Judy, you know that conversation I had with Tom, about how the golf widows would pass the time? Any thoughts?' Philip's hand hovered over the pastries and to her amusement Judy saw Roberta move very slightly to block his way.

'Yes, lots,' she said. Why did they have to discuss this now? 'There's an alpaca farm nearby, would you believe, and you can watch the wool being spun. And we wondered about hiring a mini-bus to take them to that wonderful shop in the middle of nowhere — they do clothes and antiques and there's a fabulous food hall.' Philip came over to her, nodding his approval. 'Then there's Lorn House,' Judy went on. 'It's been famous since Jacobite times. They've said they can arrange a private tour. Can we have a chat tomorrow about it?'

'I'm impressed, Judy. I think the ladies will go for all of that.' Philip followed Judy's gaze out of the window. 'It looks as if Tom could do with a hand.'

'I'm sure he'd appreciate your help,' Judy said, making her escape. She helped Corin and Verity to cover the plates of food with clingfilm and clear up. Everything seemed to be in hand now. She looked at her watch. Just the extra glasses to wash, and that might still leave her time to slip over to the annexe and change into the birthday top, because her mother was here to see her wear it.

*　*　*

The party whirled through Judy's head as she lay beside Tom, trying to sleep: Iris playing the fiddle while Donnie swung his piano accordion through traditional Scottish tunes, his foot keeping time. A hundred people talking, laughing, enjoying Corin's food. Marilyn and Roberta, sitting on a sofa, chatting nineteen to the dozen. Louise, a firefly in a short scarlet dress, seemingly everywhere at once as she held out trays of canapés and replenished glasses. Charlie slipping off to sit in the office by himself. Philip's booming voice. Herself being greeted by their guests — neighbours, bridge workers, food suppliers, people who ran local tourist attractions. Tom, as always, the perfect host. Under the bedclothes she patted his hand, although his deep breathing told her he would be unaware of the gesture.

The only casualty of the evening was the green glass vase of daisies and marigolds, knocked off the desk by a guest's shoulder-bag.

What was keeping her awake, though, was the conversation she'd overheard between Verity and a pale-faced Holly.

21

Holly looked in the mirror. The early June day wasn't quite warm enough for the blue cotton trousers but, with their drawstring waist, they were the only garment that didn't feel tight on her. A loose white top covered the incipient baby bulge.

There were still six months to go before the baby was due. She hadn't expected to grow out of her wardrobe quite so soon.

'Ready to go, sweetheart?' Corin stood at the bedroom door, car keys in hand.

'I could go on my own. I know you have a million things to do with all the bookings for tonight.'

'There is nowhere I want to be except with you and Bump.' Corin held out his hand. 'Of course I'm coming.'

In the car he buckled the seat belt for

her and planted a kiss on her cheek. 'Don't worry. Everything's going to be fine.'

'But I'm so useless,' Holly said. 'I feel I've no energy at all. We were supposed to be a team, the four of us, and I'm not fit for anything except for writing out menus and answering the phone.'

Corin started the car. 'We need someone to do both of those things, and you're very good at them.'

It was what you would say if you were placating a child. Holly turned her head away from him. Had she sounded like one?

Verity was still keen for Holly to go and stay with them in Edinburgh until she felt better. They'd almost had an argument the night of the party when Holly refused to even think about it. Apart from her role in the hotel, she certainly didn't want to be apart from Corin — and how long would it be before she felt better? After four months? Five? When the baby was born?

137

Her mother-in-law meant well, Holly knew. Her suggestion was made out of affection and genuine concern, not just for Holly herself of course but for the baby. The Grainger son and heir, as Philip referred to his future grandchild.

All that pressure and expectation from your parents on you . . . and on your partner. However awful she felt now, Holly decided that this baby would not be an only child like Corin.

She only had to wait another hour to find out that that wish had come true. The technician pointed to the undulating shapes on the screen. 'You've got two babies in there,' she said. 'Congratulations, you're having twins.'

Holly put her hand on her tummy and looked at the screen. It all became very real, and very wonderful. Two babies!

Corin grabbed her other hand and held it in both of his. Holly glanced at him. His eyes, suspiciously shiny, were riveted on the screen.

'Are they all right? Will Holly be all

right?' Holly had never heard him burble like that before.

'Everything is tickety-boo, absolutely normal,' said the technician briskly. 'We'll see you again in a few months.'

* * *

'Granmar says she can't think of any twins on her side of the family,' said Judy the next day, over elevenses.

'Verity says the same, and about Philip's too.' Who's a clever girl? was what Philip had said to Holly on the phone yesterday.

'You really have to look after yourself,' Judy said. 'Do you think,' she went on, hesitantly, 'that you should go and stay with them for a while? I heard Verity suggesting it to you.'

'No!' said Holly vehemently. 'The second three months will be better. I've been reading up about it. I should feel less tired any day now.'

'Well, take it easy today. I can hear the guests coming downstairs to check out. I'll go and see to them. Here's a stool. You put your feet up, darling.'

When Judy left the room Holly got up and put their mugs in the dishwasher. Her eye fell on the ancient, dusty, gilded soup tureen Judy had found in the back of the hall cupboard and planned to fill with flowers on the reception desk, to replace the broken glass vase. It fitted nicely into the remaining space in the dishwasher. She switched it on. No, she wasn't going to sit with her feet up and do nothing all day. She could still make a contribution.

22

Iris wiped down the last work surface and dried her hands.

'Do you know, I haven't felt sick today,' Holly said to her, looking up from the menu she was writing in her large, clear script. 'I actually feel quite normal.'

'You forget all the bad bits, even the birth, once the baby's arrived,' said Iris.

'That's what Mum says. Good to hear the same thing from someone with more recent experience! Angus is such a pet. You're a great mother, Iris. It — it must be difficult bringing him up on your own.'

Iris sat down beside Holly at the table. She'd been coming into the hotel every day for a few hours, ever since the time when Holly had emptied the dishwasher and found that the pattern had been stripped off an old china bowl. It didn't seem a big deal to Iris but apparently Holly had taken it as a sign of her general uselessness and suggested to her parents that they get outside help.

'He's an easy child.' Iris smiled at Holly. 'A happy boy. And I'm not on my own. I've got Lizzie and Roberta, and my parents, although they live down south. But . . . ' She concentrated for a moment on tracing the grain of the wooden table with her finger. Then she looked up, her smile gone. 'If Fin was still here I'd have two children to look after, not one. Life was just one long party as far as he was concerned. Irresponsible, my great-aunt Janet said. He'll never grow up. And now I can see that she was right. Great fun most of the time, film-star looks; but steady husband and father material? No. Oh, he loved Angus and me, don't get me wrong. But a proper job, staying in one place for more than a few months — he thought that was boring.'

She'd never said all that out loud

before. After the accident her family had tiptoed around her, the criticisms they'd had about Fin when he was alive silenced. She felt a kind of release now, as if getting the words out made them float away, not to trouble her again.

'Sorry,' she said, when Holly seemed to be struggling how best to respond. 'Didn't mean to burst all that out.'

'Nothing to be sorry about. What are friends for? I think you've coped so well . . . Roberta said that you'd planned to study music. Would you still like to do that?'

'I'd love to,' Iris replied, her heart warming at the thought that Holly considered her a friend. 'Playing in the hotel has made me realise again just how much. I've looked online at courses in Glasgow.' She got up from the table. 'I must pluck up the courage to have a real talk with Lizzie about the future.'

'Does she want to stay here?'

'Oh, no. She'd much rather live in the city. It's — it's hard to explain. It's not that she's bossy — well, she is a bit — but she's my big sister and thinks she knows what's best for me, and for Angus. She took care of us so well when Fin died that it's become a habit for her to make the decisions. But I don't need to be wrapped in cotton wool anymore. I want to do something with my life other than — '

'Being maid-of-all-work at the 'boat and running around after Charlie Mack?' finished Holly.

'Well, yes, if you want to put it like that. Not that I'm not grateful for the work here — '

'It's me who's grateful,' Holly said. 'My mother-in-law wanted to come and give a hand.'

'Don't you get on?' asked Iris. She kept in touch, but only intermittently, with Fin's mother, who was as nomadic as her son had been.

'Oh yes,' said Holly. 'She's lovely but she's rather scary. I can't imagine her mucking in.'

Iris laughed as she put on her jacket.

'You may need her yet. I'm going to visit my parents when the school holidays start.'

'We'll need extra staff then anyway,' said Holly. 'We're going to be pretty full, not just people to stay but coach parties for meals. And Corin wants to do afternoon teas.'

'Even if I do apply for a course it wouldn't be for this year,' Iris said. 'Too late for that. So count me in for the summer. It sounds like it's going to be a busy one. I'll see you tomorrow.'

★ ★ ★

Once Angus was in bed she'd sit down and have a frank talk with Lizzie, Iris promised herself. They would have their Saturday night glass of wine and she might even tell Lizzie what she'd told Holly. But the main thing to get across was that she was ready to move forward to the next stage of her life. Why shouldn't Lizzie give up the job she hated and go for what she wanted right now, to work in one of Glasgow's big department stores? Then Iris would follow her when, all being well, she was accepted onto a music course.

What was it Sandy had said, even as he asked her to be Charlie's home-help? Lorn is a great wee place, Iris, but there's a big world out there. You're too young to let the grass grow under your feet.

As she got within sight of Brook Cottage she realised that there was someone coming out of the gate and walking towards her: Fluffy Moustache, or whatever his name was — the bad-tempered bridge worker. Why had he been at their home?

He increased his speed, almost running. 'You're Iris, aren't you?' he asked breathlessly. He didn't look bad-tempered now, but concerned. He put his hand on her arm. 'I'm afraid your sister's had a fall.'

23

Iris started to run towards the cottage. Fluffy Moustache ran alongside gasping explanations. 'I was passing when your little lad came out of the door in quite a state. He said his Auntie Lizzie was lying on the floor and wouldn't speak to him.' He turned to look at Iris. 'She's come round now and a neighbour's with her. I phoned for an ambulance.'

'What happened?' They were almost there.

'Fell off a ladder and hit her head, I think. Let me know if there's anything I can do.'

'Thanks for all you have done.' Iris pushed open the gate. 'I don't even know your name,' she said over her shoulder as she ran down the path.

'Jim. I'm staying in . . . '

Iris didn't wait to hear.

Lizzie was still on the floor but sitting

up. Roberta had one arm round her and one around Angus, who disentangled himself, jumped up and ran over to his mother.

'Sweetheart.' Iris picked him up. 'What a brave boy you are.' Still holding him she went and knelt by Lizzie, shocked to see her sister's white face. The ladder lay beside her.

'How do you feel?' Iris asked, reaching out for Lizzie's hand.

'Woozy. But I'll be okay after a lie-down.' Lizzie tried to smile.

'You're going nowhere, young lady.' Roberta's voice was almost unrecognisably gentle. 'Any blow to the head should be checked out. We'll sit here quietly and wait for the ambulance. Iris, why don't you and Angus go and watch for it?'

Iris wanted to stay with Lizzie, but she also wanted to get Angus out of the room and blessed Roberta for allowing that to happen.

'Let's and go and look out for the nee-naw nee-naw, shall we? Maybe it will have its flashing light on.' She hoisted Angus on to her hip. 'I bet I see it first.'

'I bet I do.' Some of the usual sparkle returned to Angus's eyes as they leaned over the gate and looked down the road. They might have a long wait, Iris worried. The nearest hospital was thirty miles away, and what if the ambulances were all out on call already? She tried to remember what she knew about head injuries. Lizzie looked bad but she'd sounded quite coherent, which was good. But from what Jim said it sounded as if she'd been knocked out when she fell.

Angus wriggled and she put him down. He wasn't quite big enough to see over the gate even when he stood on tiptoe, so he bent down to peer through the spars. Iris crouched beside him and stroked the back of his head.

'Why was Auntie Lizzie up the ladder?' she asked, trying to keep her voice as neutral as possible.

'Don't know. She fell down.' Angus

pressed his face into the wooden gate.

'And what happened then?'

Angus still wouldn't look at her. 'She made a funny noise. Then it stopped. I thought Robbie would make her better.'

'So you went to find Robbie? That was clever of you.'

'The man said what's wrong, and I said Auntie Lizzie fell, and he came in and then we went to get Robbie.'

'And Robbie told him to come and find me?'

Angus took his face out of the gate so he could nod then put it back again.

'Auntie Lizzie will be all well again soon,' said Iris, hoping against hope that she was right. 'Thanks to you getting help. You've been a hero, like Superman.'

'Have I? Or Spider-Man?'

'Better than both of them. You're Superspider!' Iris was relieved to hear Angus giggle. 'Listen, Superspider, when the ambulance comes I want to go with Auntie Lizzie to the hospital. Will you stay here with Robbie?'

Angus sank back to sit on Iris's knee. 'I'll do my new trick for her.'

★ ★ ★

Iris kissed Angus goodnight and switched the bedside light off. 'See you in the morning.'

He had quite recovered his spirits by the time she'd got back, having shown Roberta his magic trick, eaten macaroni and cheese and played snap.

Now Iris sank into an armchair and smiled at her friend. 'He's none the worse. It must have given him a fright though. You've been amazing. Thank you. And Donnie.'

When Iris came out of the hospital, trying to give some thought to how she was going to get home again, there was Donnie waiting for her, sent by Roberta.

'Rubbish.' Roberta brushed her thanks aside. 'Donnie can take you in to see her tomorrow.'

Iris blinked, trying not to cry. 'They

151

said they needed to keep her in as a precaution. Do tests to check for swelling in her brain. I've phoned Mum and Dad. They're going to be here tomorrow night.'

'All for a bit of wallpaper.'

'What?'

Roberta pointed up to the corner of the room. 'The lining paper you put up and painted the other week? A bit had come unstuck and Lizzie climbed up to put it back. That ladder of yours was a health hazard. One of the steps broke.'

How the world could change in the blink of an eye.

Roberta stood up. 'Well, my dear. You know where I am. Just shout.'

'Oh.' Iris remembered. 'That man. Jim. I don't think he remembered that I'd asked him about using the hut — he's much nicer than I thought. I know you and Donnie and him don't get on but — '

'He turned up trumps today.' Roberta sat down again. 'Couldn't have been more concerned about Lizzie and

Angus. He was worried about this whole vandalism thing, I daresay. Took it out on Donnie that day. That foreman they have down there — lazy and disorganised by all accounts. I think it's your friend Jim who's really in charge.'

'Is he living in one of those caravans?' Iris asked. 'I must go and thank him.'

'Just think about Lizzie and yourself for the moment,' Roberta advised, getting to her feet once more. 'Hopefully you'll have good news to tell him soon.'

24

'One of the centre light bulbs needs replacing in the dining room,' Judy said to Tom as she whizzed past him, her arms full of bed linen.

'I could change the bulb. Granmar showed me how,' Louise said.

Judy turned back to exchange an amused look with Tom. Evidently Louise had been making herself useful at her gran's.

'I'll show you where I keep them,' Tom said.

Marilyn and Louise and Eddie had arrived the day before. Back in the B&B Louise had been a reluctant helping hand, but now she begged to be allowed to replenish the tea and coffee trays in the bedrooms and the toiletries in the en-suites. Judy was only too happy to let her.

Oh! She had a sudden thought. 'Be

careful on the ladder, Louise,' she called. 'Iris's sister fell off one and got concussion.'

As she went upstairs to join Holly in making beds, she thought it was a pity that Louise couldn't stay for the whole holiday and be proper paid help. Keep it in the family. But Louise had got herself a summer job in an art gallery owned by a friend of Marilyn's.

Iris was doing as many hours as she could, but it was difficult for her now that Angus was on school holidays and Lizzie was recuperating with their parents down south. Holly glowed with health and energy during the day but flopped in the evening. They really could do with more help if they could afford it; Tom and Judy herself were working insane hours. At least in the B&B they'd time to themselves during the day. Here, it seemed, they were never off duty.

Amazingly, while other parts of the country were being constantly rained on, the west of Scotland was enjoying dry weather and glorious sunshine. It brought the tourists in droves. Tom had hastily put up wooden tables and benches so that they could cope with the numbers wanting bar suppers, and the al fresco dining was proving popular.

'Morning, Mrs J.,' Eddie greeted her as he came down from the attic bedroom — if bedroom it could be called.

'Hope you slept well, Eddie.' It was ten o'clock, but Judy didn't mean it sarcastically. She wasn't sure how comfortable that z-bed was and she knew that Eddie had stayed up watching DVDs until very late last night. He was an owl, Louise said, while she was a lark, like Granmar.

'Great, yeah, thanks.' He gestured at the view through the landing window. 'Hey, that bridge is amazing. Can you walk across it?'

'Not yet,' Judy said. 'What are your plans for today? Maybe you and Louise could take a trip across the water on the ferry?'

'Cool. There'll be a brilliant view of the bridge from the middle of the lake

— sorry, loch. I want to draw it.'

'Good. Corin will point you in the direction of cereal and toast,' Judy said. 'Just help yourself.'

'Don't worry about me, Mrs J. I know you're well busy.'

Judy looked at his loping figure heading for the kitchen. What a nice, sensible boy he was.

'Mum, wait for me.' Louise ran through the hall. 'There's a strange mark on the dining room ceiling, as if a hole has been filled in. I want to see what it looks like in the room above.'

'Your father mentioned that. It's the bedroom on the right,' Judy said. She stood aside to let Louise past. 'I hope it's not dry rot or something. That's all we need.'

* * *

'I'm going to stay up for a bit. Me and Ed are going to play cards,' Louise said at eleven o' clock as Judy headed for bed. Tom was still in the lounge with

157

some visitors, who apparently didn't realise that hotel owners needed to sleep sometime.

'OK, sweetheart.' It would seem that Louise was an owl as well as a lark when it suited her.

Judy fell asleep instantly but half-woke when Tom slid in beside her. 'What's the time?' she asked sleepily.

'Just after one. Sorry, didn't mean to wake you.'

'Louise and Eddie still up?'

'Gone for a walk in the moonlight. I left the back door unlocked.'

'Very romantic.' *Was* there moonlight tonight? she wondered. Without it Eddie and Louise would be stumbling about in the dark. No street lights in Lorn. She dozed in and out of sleep worrying about them.

'Mum. Dad.'

Was that Louise standing by the bed whispering, or was she dreaming?

'Is something wrong?' she asked, nudging Tom at the same time.

'Me and Ed have had an adventure.

Roberta's downstairs.'

'Roberta?'

'And the police are on their way,' Louise said, forgetting to whisper.

'What! Are you all right? Is Ed OK?' Still not fully awake, Judy got out of bed and reached for her own dressing-gown and for Tom's.

''Course. We found . . . well, come down and we'll tell you.'

Judy reached for Tom's hand. What on earth had happened?

Downstairs in the kitchen Louise and Eddie burst into their story, taking turns to tell how Eddie had wanted to walk across the bridge before it was officially open and Louise suggested they try at night when there was no one around. Except there was someone. Someone throwing something off the bridge into the water. It seemed odd. Neither Louise nor Eddie had their phones with them but they saw a light on in one of the cottages and knocked . . .

'Couldn't sleep.' Roberta took up the story. 'Phoned Donnie and we went for a look. And there was the culprit of all this mischief-making. Donnie . . . '

'Donnie was great,' Eddie interrupted, his eyes glittering with excitement. 'He got hold of the guy and managed to lock him in the hut. He's keeping guard outside.'

'So was it Jim?' Tom asked. 'I wondered if he was blaming Donnie when it was actually himself.'

'No,' said Roberta as triumphantly as Hercule Poirot pointing an accusing finger in the library. 'It was the foreman, would you believe. Why? Who knows? But there's no doubt. We caught him red-handed.'

Judy looked at Eddie. So much for thinking he was a sensible boy. But Louise was just as much to blame for the escapade.

Tom seemed to be taking a different view. 'I wish I could have been there,' he said. 'Good old Donnie! I'll get dressed and go and keep him company.'

'I'll put the kettle on,' said Judy. It was going to be a long night.

25

Was it possible for a heart to sink and pound at the same time? Roberta heard Donnie open her front door and she came through from the kitchen, wondering if this time he would take 'no' as her final answer and disappear from her life. It wasn't what she wanted at all — the last thing she wanted, in fact — but she could hardly explain to herself, never mind him, why she kept putting off fixing a date for their wedding.

Ever since the vandalism mystery had been cleared up and the bridge was really taking shape under newly promoted foreman Jim's management, Donnie knew that his time as ferryman was coming to an end.

Getting married would be a good way of starting a new life — a life together, he'd told Roberta more than once, and they weren't getting any younger. What did she want, another eleven years of engagement? It would be some kind of world record.

But today he didn't have marriage on his mind, or at any rate he didn't say so. 'Guess what I've just done,' he said, looking as much like a gleeful small boy as it was possible for a ruddy-faced middle-aged man to look. Roberta's heart pounded even faster. She rubbed the finger where Donnie had placed the engagement ring eleven years ago. Why couldn't she name the day?

She tried to keep her voice steady. 'Something you shouldn't have been doing, by the sound of it.'

'Walked over to North Lorn!'

'Well you didn't walk on water I presume, so you must have been on the bridge?' *It's all right*, she thought. *We're having a normal conversation. He hasn't got tired of me prevaricating.*

'Jim says he'll take you over if you like. You can see all the way down the loch,' Donnie said enthusiastically.

Roberta nodded. 'Cool, as Eddie and Louise would say. So, it sounds as if Jim's your new best friend?'

'He's a good guy. He's asked us for a meal in his caravan on Saturday night. And . . . here's a piece of news for you. He wants to ask Lizzie as well, now that she's back to normal.'

'News! That's ancient history,' Roberta teased, quite back to normal herself now. 'When Iris went to thank him for his help he asked her all about Lizzie. Did she have a significant other? Etcetera, etcetera. Seems when he saw her lying there Sleeping Beauty came into his mind.'

'With himself as Prince Charming?' Donnie chortled. 'And how does Lizzie feel about him?'

'He called round to see her when she first came back. I would say she's interested,' Roberta said. 'Why don't you suggest to Jim that we relocate the meal to here? There can't be much room in that caravan. And it might be less awkward for him to see Lizzie on

163

neutral territory.'

'You are an old romantic after all.' Donnie planted a smacking kiss on Roberta's cheek. She held her breath but he didn't use the moment to discuss their own relationship. She said quickly in case he thought of it, 'So, Lizzie and Jim. Where does that leave Iris?'

'You're galloping ahead there, aren't you?' asked Donnie. 'They haven't even had their first date yet. Besides . . . '

'What?'

'Well, this is ancient history, as you put it, too. But I've always thought Sandy and Iris made a good pair. I've seen the way he looks at her. But he won't be her type, I suppose. He's certainly nothing like Fin.'

'She should never have married Fin. I think she knows that now. No,' Roberta said, shaking her head vigorously as Donnie opened his mouth to speak, 'she never said that. Not in so many words. But I can read between the lines. He was exciting and glamorous, in the eyes of a young girl. She got carried away, almost literally. Getting married was just a lark for him, I think. She'll never regret it because of Angus, of course, but I think she's ready to move on.'

'Roberta Roberts, agony aunt,' Donnie mocked gently.

'Hah, that'll be the day.' Roberta changed the subject. 'Jim say anything about the trial? You'll be called as a witness of course.'

'It's a slow process, won't be for months yet. Yes, star witness for the prosecution. Not looking forward to that. Jim thinks that idiot had money problems and wanted to delay finishing the bridge in case he didn't have another project to go to.' He looked at his watch. 'Must go. I'll fix it up with Jim for Saturday. And you'll ask Lizzie? See you later, Ro.'

Roberta watched him go down the path, Iris still on her mind. She was old enough to be Iris's mother, but there was a very solid friendship between them that Roberta did not want to jeopardise. Neither, though, did she want to stand back and see Iris not doing more with her life, whether that involved realising her potential as a musician or forming a happy, grown-up relationship. Or both. She wasn't sure what she could do about the first except be encouraging about college applications; but maybe she could, tactfully of course, interfere a little to try to bring about the second.

'Sandy makes me laugh,' Iris had said. That was a good basis for a partnership. He had probably heard through Charlie about Lizzie's accident, maybe even been in touch with Iris about it. But there would be no harm in Roberta taking it upon herself to keep Sandy up to date with the latest news — and somehow give a little hint that he might try to rekindle his teenage romance with Iris.

She'd pop down to Charlie's later and find out how to contact Sandy. Nothing ventured, nothing gained.

She pushed her own potential partnership to the back of her mind.

26

Iris brought in the lunch dishes from the garden and stacked them in the dishwasher. 'That's it,' she said, switching it on.

'How many today?' Holly asked. She was sitting at the kitchen table with her sewing machine, running up curtains for the annexe.

'Don't know,' Iris said, counting on her fingers. 'But . . . two, five, nine . . . there must have been fourteen outside, and the dining room was full.'

Verity, enveloped in a rosy Cath Kidston apron, looked up from the mixing bowl. 'Are you off now, Iris? Holly and I are on afternoon teas.'

'Yes, I'll be back in the evening.' Iris smiled at Mrs Grainger senior, or Verity, as she'd been told to call her.

She'd been surprised, and suspected that the Jeffreys were too, at how good

Verity was at mucking in with whatever required to be done. She'd been here, on and off, for the last few weeks and Iris wondered how they could possibly have managed without her. She knew that Holly had been rather dreading seeing so much of her mother-in-law, but it seemed to Iris that they were getting on well.

She walked slowly home, enjoying the sunshine and the view of the purple hills above the loch. Sandy had emailed to ask how Lizzie was and to say that tomorrow, Friday, he was coming to stay with Charlie for the weekend. So that was something to look forward to. Everyone had been so kind — their sitting-room was still full of the flowers Lizzie had received, including a beautiful arrangement from Sandy.

She turned the corner. Sandy was getting out of a car.

Seeing him unexpectedly was disconcerting, almost as if she were seeing a stranger. He was a tall, broad-shouldered man in jeans and a white shirt, stretching his back after a long drive, pushing his fair hair out of his eyes. But when he turned and saw her, his face breaking into a smile, there was her old friend Sandy, so familiar and reassuring, so *real*, that she ran forward to greet him.

He knew the facts about Lizzie's fall, of course, but she longed suddenly to tell him how she had felt when it happened. Lizzie was much better now and would be ready to go back to work next week. The hospital had given her a clean bill of health. But Iris couldn't get out of her mind the sight of her sister lying so still and so white, and she couldn't bear to think of Angus seeing her like that too.

It was frightening to remember that accidents could happen so quickly; how short life could be . . . But it was funny too, the way things had turned out. It seemed that Jim (she must stop thinking of him as Fluffy Moustache) was keen on Lizzie, and as her sister went pink when his name was mentioned it would appear the feeling was mutual.

'I thought you weren't coming until tomorrow,' Iris said.

'Managed to get away early and grabbed a flight cancellation. Hey, come here. You need a hug. Bad time, eh?'

'Yes,' Iris said, her voice muffled against his chest. She couldn't be sure but she thought he dropped a light kiss on the top of her head. 'Lizzie's fine now,' she said, blinking in the sunlight as he released her. 'There she is at the window.'

Sandy returned Lizzie's wave. 'I hear love is in the air.'

'Who told you that? The Lorn bush telegraph travels far! Yes, Lizzie's really happy. Jim's a bit older than her but they seem to have a lot in common. Are you coming in?'

'Thanks, yes, I'd like to see Lizzie. Angus at school, I expect?'

'Yes. He'll be thrilled you're here. Prepare yourself for a magic show before you leave.'

'Nothing I'd like better! Well, almost nothing.' He caught her arm as they walked down the path. 'We never really got a chance to catch up when I was here back in March. Are you free tomorrow night? Shall we hit the bright lights of Oban?'

'I'm not working tomorrow, but what about Charlie?'

'Don't worry about Uncle Charlie. I'll make him a nice meal before I go out. Will Lizzie be here to look after Angus?'

'No, she and Jim and Roberta and Donnie are going to a ceilidh in North Lorn. But Angus is staying with one of the little boys from his class tomorrow night, his first sleepover. He's really excited.'

'So that's a yes, then?'

'That's a yes.'

* * *

Angus looked at Sandy's bowl of mussels with wide-eyed interest before turning his attention to his own plate piled high with smoked salmon and bread and butter.

'Look,' Iris said, 'you can take this piece of lemon and squeeze it over.' She exchanged a smiling glance with Sandy as the little boy carefully dropped juice on each piece of salmon.

Plans for the evening had changed. Just as Sandy arrived, another car stopped at Iris's gate. Angus's friend had got back from school feeling sick apparently and, as he hadn't improved, his mum drove Angus home.

Iris offered to cook something for Sandy but he wouldn't hear of it, declaring that Angus deserved a night out too and tomorrow wasn't a school day. In Oban they'd walked up to Macaig's Folly and now they were sitting in a restaurant with a wonderful view over the bay.

Iris wondered what Sandy had meant by a 'catch-up'. If he wanted to look back at the summer of their brief romance and how it ended, then obviously with Angus there that wasn't going to happen.

Besotted with Fin as she'd been, Iris was afraid, with hindsight, that she hadn't let Sandy down as gently as she might. But they were just teenagers then; their relationship probably didn't mean anything to Sandy now other than part of growing up. And Iris didn't want to talk about that time and her subsequent marriage to Fin anyway. Sometimes it seemed like a dream, or as if it had happened to someone else.

So she smiled brightly and updated Sandy on Lorn news, and he told them about where he lived in Zurich and about climbing in the Alps whenever he got the chance.

When Angus finished eating he went to look out of the picture window at the boats.

There must be a girl in Sandy's life, Iris thought. *Just because he hasn't mentioned one doesn't mean . . .* Surely it shouldn't be difficult to ask her childhood friend if he was seeing someone? But somehow it was. Anyway, she would just enjoy the moment now when he and she were here, and Switzerland was far away, and . . .

'Why don't you and Angus come out for a holiday?' Sandy interrupted her thoughts. 'I have a spare room in my lonely bachelor flat. There's lots to do — and the music college has great concerts.'

So there was the answer to the question she hadn't asked. 'Well, I . . . ' She concentrated on eating the last mouthful of salad, playing for time.

'Look, no strings attached, if that's what you're thinking,' he said, touching her arm briefly. 'We're old friends, aren't we? You could do with a break. And I'd like your company, and Angus's.'

'Can I think about it? It wouldn't be until the end of the season.'

'Of course. The offer will stay open.' He grinned at her. 'Now, do you think Angus would like some ice cream?'

27

There were times when Tom wished himself back in Harpenden and the B&B. He wondered if Judy felt the same but didn't want to say. That maybe they'd bitten off more than they could chew.

They'd been so busy since they moved north — the eight months seemed to have gone by in a blur of hard physical work punctuated by sleep. Ideally they would have taken on another pair of hands, but Tom was trying to cut their costs as much as possible.

So he felt almost guilty when he found himself in town with an hour to kill while the garage sorted out a problem with the car. He only hoped it wouldn't take longer than promised. The repair couldn't be delayed — they couldn't do without the car — but the timing was bad. Corin was having a much-needed evening off and he and Holly were on their way to Glasgow to meet up with old friends. He'd delegated tonight's dinner, adjusting his menu for one that was less complicated, but Tom knew Judy was rather nervous about being left in charge.

Tom wished Judy and he could have some time off together. She was looking so tired — with work, and also because of worrying if Marilyn would be lonely when Louise went away to university. Personally, Tom thought she'd be just fine. She had so many friends and interests — but in Judy's eyes that didn't make up for the family being so far away.

If Judy were here now, Tom thought, they would stroll along looking in all the café windows, choosing one to sit down in and have a cup of tea and talk about anything but work. But there was just himself and, try as he might to avoid it, all he could think about was the hotel.

Verity had turned out to be a great asset, able to pick up the slack wherever it might be. The drawback of having her around was seeing more of Philip — he insisted on taking her over from Edinburgh and picking her up again a few days later when she was perfectly capable of driving herself. But he was 'keeping an eye on his investment' and Tom could hardly avoid him.

Then there were the forthcoming babies — delightful though the prospect of them was, there was the problem of space. Corin and Holly could hardly be expected to share a room in the annexe with their offspring forever, and each room in the hotel had to earn its keep.

But — he put up his hand to shade his eyes from the sun — there was the water in Oban Bay sparkling in front of him, a sprinkling of bright yacht sails on the horizon. What a beautiful part of the world. Worth all the graft to have this on your doorstep.

He realised he was passing the Visitors' Centre and decided to pop in to check that they hadn't run out of Ferryboat leaflets.

'It's Mr Jeffrey, isn't it?' It was the assistant who had been friendly and helpful the first time he'd come in.

'Tom,' he said.

'How's business?'

'Pretty good.' Tom nodded. 'Town looks busy.'

'This sunny spell has brought every-one to the west, it seems. A bumper season. I've heard great things about your son-in-law's cooking.' She smiled. 'I must come out and sample it.'

'You do that,' Tom said heartily. It was great to have confirmation that in a short time Corin was garnering a good reputation for the Ferryboat.

'Oh, talking of food,' she said, 'I've heard a rumour that — '

'Tom! Fancy meeting you here.'

Tom turned to see Charlie grinning at him from under a jaunty cap.

'Saw you coming in,' Charlie said.

'I've just been for a sail round the bay with a pal.'

'You're looking well,' Tom said.

'Getting used to this retirement lark now. Have bus pass, will travel. I promised Sandy I wouldn't let myself get down in the dumps again.'

'Good stuff,' said Tom. It was ridiculous but he had been feeling guilty about Charlie's bad spell, as if he'd stolen the hotel from under his nose. 'I can give you a lift back if you like.' He turned back to the assistant. 'I'm sorry,' he said, 'what were you going to say?'

'The rumour is,' she said, 'that Andrea Gilmore — you know, the restaurant reviewer for one of the Sundays — is up here and doing the rounds.'

'Oh ho,' said Charlie. 'Rather you than me, Tom. I read her every week. That woman does not mince her words.'

She was sure to love Corin's food, thought Tom. And a great review in a national newspaper, even Philip would be pleased with.

His phone buzzed in his pocket. Probably the garage telling him the car was ready. 'Excuse me,' he said, and he walked to the other end of the room to take the call.

'Tom?' Judy sounded on the verge of tears. 'When will you be back? We have a problem.'

28

Tom grabbed Charlie's arm. 'That Gilmore woman. She's booked into the Ferryboat for dinner tonight. Iris recognised her name. And — '

'I don't think you've anything to worry about.' The soothing voice of the Visitor Centre lady broke in on his babble. 'Your son-in-law's cooking — '

'He's not there,' Tom said. 'He's having a night off. Of all the nights . . . Charlie, are you coming? I must get home.'

With a wave of goodbye he ushered Charlie out of the door and round the corner to the garage. 'Corin's in Glasgow — Judy's trying to get hold of him. He's not answering his phone.'

'Calm down, Tom.' Charlie stopped to catch his breath before increasing his speed to catch up.

'Calm down? This is either the best

or the worst thing that's happened since we bought the Ferryboat, and we'll soon find out which.' It was different for Charlie. He'd been running what was basically a pub with rooms — how could he understand about fine dining and aiming for a Michelin star and everything they had staked their family's future on?

Nodding at what he hoped were suitable intervals, he tuned out Charlie's voice as he negotiated the car through Oban and concentrated on getting to Lorn in the fastest possible time allowed by the speed limit.

About halfway down the road his phone rang. 'Could you answer that, Charlie?' he asked, indicating where it sat on the shelf in front of the passenger seat. 'I don't want to stop.'

Charlie fumbled with the buttons. 'Judy? It's Charlie, speaking on behalf of your good man who's driving like Jehu to get back to you.' He turned to wink at Tom. 'Can I give him a message — ? Uh-huh. Will do. So you're in charge? What's on the menu?' He listened intently to Judy's answer.

Tom gripped the steering wheel. Was Charlie expecting to be invited to dinner? To sit in the dining room alongside Andrea Gilmore?

'Lovely, Judy. Don't worry, we're on our way.' Charlie pressed the red button to end the call. 'Still no word from Corin. She's left four messages now. And Holly's not picking up either.'

'Judy, Verity, Iris, me,' Tom thought aloud. 'It would be do-able, a full dining-room, under normal circumstances. But with that woman . . . Corin would have pulled out all the stops.'

'Well, he's not going to be there,' Charlie said. 'It sounds as if he left Judy instructions for some very do-able, as you put it, dishes which all sound just the job. And with the view from the dining room window, and a glass of something from your excellent cellar, Miss Gilmore will be on her knees begging to stay for a week.'

'I like your optimism,' Tom said,

smiling in spite of himself. To distract himself from the problem he said, 'Charlie, been meaning to ask. In the dining room ceiling there's a place where it looks as if a plug of wood has been put in, and — '

'You haven't heard the old yarn about the place? I always meant to make some kind of a feature of it. Maybe you will.' Charlie settled back in his seat and put on a jokey pirate's accent.

'It's all to do with smugglers, Tom lad,' he said. 'The story goes that the excise men — customs as we would say now — relieved some smugglers of a cask of whisky made illegally up in the hills. They spent the night at the Ferryboat, in a first-floor bedroom, the cask in with them. In the middle of the night the smugglers crept in and persuaded the chambermaid to tell them which room the men were in, and whereabouts on the floor the cask was. They drilled a hole in the ceiling of what is now your dining room, drained the whisky into another cask and were miles away by morning.'

'That's wonderful.' Tom smacked the steering wheel in delight. 'I'd never have guessed that was the explanation.' He must ask Louise to design a plaque telling the story — it would be a real talking point in the dining room. His distraction idea was so successful that the fact that an influential restaurant reviewer was coming for dinner only rushed back into his head as he passed the sign for Lorn.

'Where are you going?' Charlie asked, as Tom signalled left to go up the hill.

'I'll drop you off,' Tom said. Where did Charlie think he was going?

'No, no. It's all hands on deck at the old Ferry tonight. I'll come in with you.'

Tom was touched. 'Good of you, Charlie, but — '

'I suspected you weren't listening earlier.' Charlie grinned. 'I was saying I haven't always served up microwaved grub. Back in the day I worked with a top-notch chef in London for a year. Had to come home when my dad got ill. Still remember a few tricks of the trade though.' He was out of the car as soon as Tom cut the engine, moving across the yard as if he'd shed twenty years.

Judy was at the cooker, peering into a saucepan. She looked at them over her shoulder, her eyes widening when she saw Charlie.

'Corin just called,' she said. 'They left their phones inside while they sat in their friends' garden. He said they'll come back, but what's the point? It's six now, and by the time they get here . . . ' She stopped and stared at Charlie as he put on an apron and went to the sink to wash his hands.

'Tell me what to do, Mrs J.,' he said. 'I'm your commis chef for the night.'

Behind Charlie's back Tom nodded at Judy, who evidently decided to keep her questions for later. She relinquished her place at the cooker. 'That's the redcurrant sauce for the venison,' she said. 'Hollandaise for the salmon there, tarragon to be added. Tartiflette potatoes ready to go in the oven. If only we knew what Andrea Gilmore is going to order . . . '

★ ★ ★

'Ceviche of halibut and the venison steak, medium rare,' reported Verity, coming back from the dining room.

'Good choice,' Charlie said approvingly. 'She wants to see he can do innovative dishes and not mess up the short-order ones.'

'Except 'he' isn't here,' said Judy, remembering the melt-in-the-mouth venison steaks Corin had made on their first night.

'Leave the steak to me,' said her commis chef, and Judy took him at his word and went to arrange the fish and its accompaniments on a plate as Corin had shown her.

There were other guests' starters to

deliver too, of course. Following Corin's instructions to the letter, Judy and Iris got through them while Tom dealt with the wine orders. Judy was aware of Charlie, steaks lined up, warmed plates at hand, looking very relaxed. What was the story, she wondered, behind his heaven-sent appearance in the kitchen?

'Our VIP said her steak was excellent,' Verity said later with a smile as she brought back an empty plate. Charlie's smile stretched from ear to ear and Judy blew him a kiss.

'She'd like the trio of raspberry puds,' Verity added.

Judy was in her comfort zone now, and though she said so herself, the three desserts looked beautiful on the rose-patterned plate.

Andrea Gilmore had just asked for her bill when Corin and Holly burst into the kitchen. Verity came back after taking the payment. 'She wants to pay her compliments to the chef,' she said in a horrified whisper, relief flooding into her face when she saw her son.

'What did she eat?' Corin asked, throwing on his white jacket, and Verity told him before he went through to the dining room.

Holly sat down rather heavily at the table. 'I was afraid I was going to go into labour ten weeks early the rate Corin was driving. Phew, glad we got here in time. Although it should be you, Mum, taking the credit.'

Judy swept her arm round the room to indicate Iris, Verity and Charlie. 'A team effort,' she said, 'including a brilliant commis chef.'

29

'Have you been speaking to Sandy lately?' Roberta asked. She felt a little guilty about questioning Angus, but Iris seemed to change the subject now when Sandy's name was mentioned.

'We've seen him!' Angus said excitedly, to Roberta's surprise. 'We got Skype! It's like magic, isn't it?'

'Indeed it is.' Although she didn't think she cared for the idea of having it herself. She would always feel that she had to brush her hair and tidy the room first — you didn't have to worry about that before making an ordinary phone call. She got up from the path to stretch her back.

'I did Sandy my hanky trick,' Angus went on, 'and he showed us the view out his window.'

'That was nice.' Brilliant, in fact.

Things seemed to be moving along with Iris and Sandy.

Angus looked up at her from where he crouched down, industriously watering plants with his little can. 'Sandy said to come to Switzerland for a holiday but Mummy said no.'

'Why did she say that?' Roberta asked, feeling as disappointed as if she'd been rejected herself.

But Angus had turned back to the flowerbed. 'Look, Robbie, a worm!' He plunged his fingers into the earth. He had always loved the wriggly creatures in Roberta's garden and gave them names, maintaining that he recognised them from one visit to the next. He'd been fascinated when Roberta told him that worms were both girl and boy.

Roberta knelt down again, her knees going back into the dents in her old tweed skirt. 'Is that Wendy-and-Walt — ?' She stopped. In one grubby hand Angus clutched a worm — and something else.

He transferred Wendy-and-Walter to

his other hand and dropped a ring onto Roberta's outstretched palm. 'It's a treasure,' he said.

Slowly, Roberta rubbed the ring against her skirt to loosen the dirt. She put it on her engagement finger and held up her hand to look at it. Sunlight caught the emerald and the diamonds on either side of it and they glinted at her. She felt very peculiar, but in a good way, the way you feel when you're getting back to normal after a bout of flu.

'Angus, come on.' She jumped up. 'We must go and see Donnie right now. Take Wendy-and-Walter with you if you want.'

Her skirt retained the bulges where her knees had been, and had a dirty mark from the earth rubbed off the ring. She scorned wearing gardening gloves so her fingernails showed how she'd spent the morning. But she wasn't about to waste time beautifying herself.

The ring was back on her finger where it belonged, and Donnie had waited for her answer long enough.

30

'For the actual ceremony it's only going to be themselves, Donnie's brother and me,' Iris told Holly, 'then back to the Ferry for the meal and the dance. Lizzie says she can come up beforehand, if that's any help, although she'll have Angus with her. If she's still here, that is.'

'That would be great,' Holly said. 'And I'm sure we can find something to keep Angus amused.' She rubbed her hand over her bump. 'If these two are poppets like Angus we'll be very lucky.'

'Do you know . . . ' Iris began.

'Whether they're boys or girls?' Holly finished. She laughed. 'Yes, but I'm not saying. Mum and Dad and Granmar want it to be a surprise, so Corin and I haven't told anyone. Philip's been trying to find out — thinks we should be putting their names down for schools before they're even born. Did you ever hear the like? But he'll have to wait like everyone else.'

'So.' Iris reverted to talking about the wedding. 'Have Roberta and Donnie chosen a menu?'

'All sorted,' Holly confirmed. 'Our first wedding. It's so exciting. What will Roberta be wearing?'

Iris groaned. 'Her gardening clothes, if she had her way. No, really, she absolutely hates clothes shopping. Lizzie and I are taking her to Glasgow one day next week to force her to buy something. I can't say I'm looking forward to it.'

Holly laughed. 'It's so funny the way you told it, about the ring being found. Roberta marching down to Donnie's, bits of earth sticking to the diamonds, Angus in tow . . . '

'Don't forget the pet worm.' It made Iris giggle even six weeks on to imagine the funny little procession heading purposefully down to the cottage by the ferry. Angus had had no idea why

Roberta suddenly decided to visit Donnie at that moment, and he didn't care — all he was thinking about was taking the worm on an adventure. What happened when they'd reached Donnie's house Iris could only speculate.

Donnie and Roberta had brought Angus home — on his own, Wendy-and-Walter having been mislaid somewhere along the way — longing to tell someone their news.

'She's set a date at last, Iris,' Donnie had said, his face glowing. 'At least, one we hope the registrar and the hotel will agree with. Then she'll be Roberta Campbell and we'll live happily ever after.'

'Only reason I'm doing it,' Roberta joked, but with a catch in her voice. 'To stop being Roberta Roberts.'

Now Iris remembered their joy and that phrase of Donnie's, unoriginal though it was — 'happily ever after' — and felt her eyes prickle with tears.

'I can't imagine being engaged for eleven years, can you?' Holly asked.

'The minute Corin sat beside me on that flight from Spain I knew he was the one. And he felt the same. We were married less than a year later. Mum and Dad thought we should wait, but you just know, don't you?' She was clearly in a rosy reminiscent glow, forgetting that Iris had also married young and that had not ended happily.

Even when Fin was alive Iris had found it hard to imagine growing old with him. He was so carefree, always living in the moment. It was exhilarating to be around someone like that when you were barely out of your teens, but probably he wouldn't have changed no matter what life threw at them over the years. The word 'irresponsible' slipped disloyally into her head. She pushed it away. *Fin's gone*, Iris told herself. *He's never coming back. And I have the rest of my life to live.*

Holly pulled a chair round so that she could put her feet up on it. 'And what about Lizzie and Jim? Wedding bells there?'

'Definitely ringing in the distance,' Iris said, tearing her mind from the past. 'Jim will be moving on when the bridge is finished and she'll be going with him.' She changed the subject in case Holly, in the mood for romantic gossip, should turn her attention to Iris herself. 'So, what's planned for the bridge opening next month?'

'There's a lunch to be laid on for the MP who's cutting the ribbon, and for the other dignitaries. And at night, not an arranged party as such, but I imagine we'll be pretty busy. Dad's hiring a couple of extra bar staff for the evening and we're doing a free buffet for the bridge workers. We've had such a lot of custom from them. It will be quiet when they're not here anymore.'

It will be quiet at Brook Cottage too, thought Iris. *Just Angus and me when Lizzie goes. Roberta will still be across the road, but she'll probably have less time for us when Donnie's moved in. I must speak to Judy and see how much work she thinks there'll be for me here over the winter. And I should do something else, an online music course maybe* . . . The idea didn't exactly set her pulses racing.

She could have had a holiday in Switzerland to look forward to — Sandy had mentioned it again since their evening in Oban, asking what date Angus's October school holidays were and saying he'd arrange to take time off. Angus always sat with her when they spoke to Sandy on Skype and bounced with excitement at the idea of flying to Switzerland. It was hard to deny him and hard, too, to look Sandy in the eye and prevaricate. Sometimes she wondered that perhaps if Angus wasn't beside her that their conversation might have taken a different turn, but that was wishful thinking — there were other methods of communication after all.

As she walked home she thought about Roberta and Donnie — like Holly, she couldn't imagine being engaged for eleven years. The future was bright for them, but what a lot of time they had wasted.

Sandy had never indicated that they might take up where they left off when Fin had swept them apart; not in words, anyway. There was just a feeling in the air the last time he was home, and when they faced each other via the computer screen — as if he were trying to communicate something to her that he was afraid to spell out but hoped she would respond to favourably. She had let him down once before after all. Or maybe she was imagining it and he just wanted them to be friends and to be a kind of uncle figure to Angus.

There was only one way to find out. Not the right time for skyping — Sandy would be at work. And it would be better anyway if she emailed, taking time to think about what to say.

Dear Sandy, she typed, *I don't think I ever said I was sorry for leaving you the way I did. I've often wished since that I'd done it differently — told you face to face. A kind of recklessness took over, which isn't really me at all. Of course it happened years ago and we were so young and you may not have given it another thought! But it's been on my mind and if it's not too late, I'm saying sorry now. Iris.*

She pressed Send before she lost courage.

Five minutes later the phone rang. 'Iris?' Sandy's voice came through a blur of background noise. 'I've got a meeting in two minutes. Just read your email.'

'I wasn't sure — '

'You've nothing to apologise for.'

Iris tried to picture where he might be, sitting at his desk or leaning against a wall in a corridor maybe, pushing his fair hair out of his eyes, his phone pressed close to his ear.

'Listen,' said Sandy, 'you know what I said, in Oban, about no strings attached? What an idiot! I want strings. Lots of them. I want us to be together. You and me and Angus. Will you — '

He broke off to speak to someone else.

'Yup, on my way, give me a minute. Iris, I'm down on one knee here. Will you marry me?'

Her heart felt as if it had jumped into her throat and her voice sounded croaky. 'Yes.' She said it again in case he hadn't heard her. 'Yes.'

'She said yes!' There were sounds of whooping and cheering at the other end of the line.

'I never stopped loving you,' Sandy said, so softly she could hardly hear him — words for her alone and not his audience. 'There was never anyone but you.'

31

'What's the damage this month?' Judy looked over Tom's shoulder as he did the hotel's accounts.

'Oh there's damage, but we're on track. Just over a year since we first considered coming here, and we haven't lost as much money as I was afraid we would.'

'I take it that's good news.' Judy leaned her chin on his head. 'Although it sounds gloomy.'

'The review's been a big help.' Tom remembered that hectic evening and Andrea Gilmore's subsequent five-star endorsement, which he credited with bringing them diners from far afield and enquiries for weddings and other functions well into the next year. 'And now the bridge is open there's lots more passing traffic. Of course there'll be rent to pay on Brook Cottage from

November,' he added. 'That can't be helped. But the timing couldn't be better.'

With herself headed for a new life in Zurich and Lizzie preparing to move north with Jim, and neither of them wanting to sell the cottage their great-aunt had left them, Iris had asked if Holly and Corin might want to take a long lease on it. The Graingers and the Jeffreys fell on the suggestion gratefully. It would be a perfect home, just down the road from the hotel, to bring the babies back to.

'So.' Judy's voice was mischievous. 'Are you looking forward to this afternoon?'

Tom covered his face with his hands in mock horror. 'Maybe he'll phone and cancel,' he said hopefully.

'No chance,' said Judy. 'Not after all the fuss he's made. Besides, he texted Corin five minutes ago to say he was just leaving.' She planted a kiss on his cheek. 'No pressure, but the honour of the Jeffreys is at stake.'

'If you've nothing helpful to say, go away,' Tom growled, and with a laugh Judy went.

Philip had worn Tom down until he had eventually agreed to have a game of golf with him before winter set in. It was to take place on the course nearest to Lorn with which Philip and his cronies had got well acquainted. Tom had only managed a couple of rounds — but he did have an ace up his sleeve . . .

★ ★ ★

'I know you haven't played much,' Philip said, shutting the door of his silver Audi, 'so what I propose is that I give you a stroke a hole.'

The golfing equivalent of a head start. 'No, you're all right, Philip.' Tom lifted his golf bag out of the boot. 'Let's start on equal terms. Make more of a game of it.'

Philip slapped him on the back. 'Well, don't say I didn't offer. That's an impressive set of clubs you've got there.' He bent to make a closer inspection.

'Yes.' Tom looked up at the sky to deflect Philip's attention. 'Don't like the look of those clouds. Let's get on.'

Philip pushed his tee into the ground. 'The first hole is tricky,' he said, standing up again. 'It's a long one between the bunkers. Into the wind, too. I'll go first, shall I?'

Show me how it's done, you mean, Tom thought. He held up his hand to shade his eyes. 'Good shot.' It was too. Philip was a worthy opponent.

In his turn he lifted his club and sliced the ball down the fairway.

'Tom! Well done you.' Philip's tone didn't match his words. Looking rather annoyed, he picked up his bag and strode off.

Three quarters of the way through the course, Tom putted the ball across the green and both men watched as it fell neatly into the hole.

'I think you've been holding out on me,' Philip said as Tom went to retrieve it. 'Have you been taking lessons from Tiger Woods?'

'I wish,' Tom laughed. 'You're right, though. I may have forgotten to mention that before we went into the B&B business I was a professional for ten years. At the Ashbridge course — you've probably heard of it.'

Philip whistled. 'I certainly have.' Various emotions crossed his face. Then he burst out laughing and held out his hand. 'It's not often someone gets one over on me.'

Tom shook the proffered hand heartily. 'No hard feelings, I hope.'

'Not at all. Delighted to think that our grandsons, if they are grandsons, will have a head start with both you and me to teach them,' Philip said. He put his club back in his bag. 'You're right, Tom. I think it is going to rain. Shall we call it a day and repair to the clubhouse? I'm sure you have some cracking stories to tell.'

Tom turned away to hide his smile. Philip didn't want to finish the game and admit defeat, but they both knew who was the winner today.

32

Judy stood at the front door of the Ferryboat to welcome Mr and Mrs Donald Campbell. Roberta looked striking in a deep red dress and little hat on her iron-grey hair. Iris must have persuaded her to have a manicure in addition to her hairdresser's appointment, because the hand she thrust out to show Judy her wedding ring was tipped red at the end.

'Mummy!' Angus shot through the hall into Iris's arms. 'Me and Sandy have been helping.'

'I can see what you've been doing,' Iris laughed, taking out a tissue and wiping his mouth. 'Sampling the wedding lunch.'

She looked a completely different woman from the one Judy had first met — standing taller, her face in what seemed to be a permanent smile. The cause of her happiness followed behind Angus.

'How did it go?' Sandy asked.

'It was lovely,' Iris said. 'Very special.' She put Angus back on his feet.

Roberta put her hand on Angus's head. 'You look smashing in your kilt,' she said. 'Oh, I am going to miss you. All those bulbs you helped to plant. You won't be here to see them grow.'

Charlie came forward, wanting to be among the first to congratulate the newlyweds in his own way. 'You caught her at last, Donnie boy!' he said, clapping his old friend on the shoulder. He turned to beam on Sandy, Iris and Angus — his new little family.

Judy ushered the wedding party into the dining room to be greeted by the rest of their guests including Marilyn, invited by Roberta because they had got on so well at the hotel's opening party. And, primed by Judy, Roberta was going to ask Marilyn a question which Judy thought might be better posed by someone other than herself.

The bride stood by her chair and kicked off her high heels before she sat down. She sighed with relief and then removed her hat. 'Stick that somewhere for me, Judy, would you, please? Right, I can enjoy myself now, especially as I see your husband approaching with the champagne.'

To loud applause Donnie stood up and said that he and his wife were very pleased to see them all and hoped they would enjoy the dinner and the rest of the evening.

Judy retreated to the kitchen to help with the serving of the meal. 'Where's Holly?' she asked Corin.

Holly had designed the menus and place-name cards — something she could do sitting down — and when Judy had last seen her she was putting the final touches to the wedding cake decorations.

'She finished the cake and went to have a lie-down,' Corin said. 'She's really tired — those are bouncing babies we're having! OK, I'm ready, Judy, let's get this show on the road.'

* * *

Marilyn came through the swing door into the kitchen. 'What a gorgeous dinner,' she said. 'Three cheers for the chef, wherever he is.' She went over to where Judy was making coffee and put her arm around her daughter's shoulders. 'Roberta says that the ferryman's cottage is up for sale and why didn't I think about buying it.'

Judy held her breath, uncertain now whether it would be a good idea for Marilyn to leave all her long-time friends and social activities and move north to a very different lifestyle.

'Did you put her up to it? Nice try,' Marilyn said.

'It's a perfect size for one person, and with Louise at university now I thought . . . ' Judy began.

'I know. And it was a lovely thought.'

Marilyn shook her immaculately coiffured head. 'When I'm old I promise you I'll head for the hills and you and Tom. But not yet. Not while — ' She stopped as Corin hurtled through the back door.

'I went to see Holly,' he said. 'This shouldn't be happening for two weeks yet but she says the babies are on their way.'

★   ★   ★

'She's absolutely perfect.' Verity looked down at the baby in her arms. She lowered her voice. 'Is this Kathleen or Fiona?'

'Kathleen,' Judy whispered back. 'But I only know because Holly said she'd dressed her in a lemon babygro. Fiona's is white. I can't tell them apart otherwise.'

Their eyes met in mutual adoration of the little girls, now a week old and sleeping through their first evening out of hospital.

'Is Philip disappointed there isn't a boy?' Judy asked, her voice still quiet.

'He is as thrilled as I am with our granddaughters,' said Verity. She glanced up to where her husband cradled the other baby.

Philip caught a tiny flailing arm gently in his big hand. 'Did you see that, Tom? That's a golfer's swing. Winner of the Women's Open one day! That would be something, wouldn't it?'

'It certainly would.' Out of Philip's sight Tom gave Judy a mock grimace. But Judy looked at Philip with affection, having seen his eyes shiny with love for the new arrivals.

I must get up, there's so much to do, Judy thought, but for the moment the armchair was just too comfortable and she could hardly tear herself away from the babies.

There was always so much to do in the hotel, twenty-four hours a day, seven days a week. She and Tom were going away for a week's holiday in January when the hotel was closed, so that was something to look forward to. But before that they were fully booked for Christmas and New Year, and Louise and Marilyn would be coming up — would it be fair to ask Corin and Holly if they could stay at Brook Cottage with them? she worried.

Tom was still making faces at her. She tuned back in to hear Philip saying, 'And we really want to be on hand to help and not miss this pair growing up, so . . . ' He paused dramatically. 'We're hoping to buy the ferryman's little cottage and come over here as often as we can.'

Judy felt a stab of disappointment that it was not going to be Marilyn, the twins' great-grandmother, who would be near them, part of all their lives.

'And you must consider the cottage as yours too,' Verity added. 'Anytime your mother or Louise come up they'd be very welcome to stay in it.'

Tom had turned away and Judy knew he was composing himself to look pleased. She leaned over to squeeze

Verity's hand to make up for his lack of response. 'That's wonderful,' she said. 'Isn't it, Tom?'

Her dear Tom rose to the occasion. 'I think I could get used to the idea,' he said. 'Give Philip the chance to up his game and beat me on the golf course.'

Philip began to guffaw but stopped himself in case he woke Fiona.

Judy exchanged raised eyebrows with Verity. 'Boys will be boys,' she said as she pushed herself up from the chair. 'I'll make some tea, shall I?'

Grinning at Tom, she went through to the kitchen where Holly was sitting at the table leaning tiredly against Corin, having a quiet moment before taking their babies home to Brook Cottage.

'Philip and Verity have just told us they're planning to buy the ferryman's house,' Judy said.

'How do you feel about that?' Corin had a twinkle in his eye.

'It's great news,' said Judy firmly, and she meant it. Because, whatever their differences, she and Tom and Philip and Verity were bound together through Holly and Corin, and even more now through Kathleen and Fiona, and family was what mattered most. Each of them had come a long way in the past year, in all sorts of ways.

As she pulled down the blinds she saw the sliver of new moon illuminating the hotel sign.

The Ferryboat.

Home.

THE END

We do hope that you have enjoyed reading this large print book.

Did you know that all of our titles are available for purchase?

We publish a wide range of high quality large print books including:
Romances, Mysteries, Classics
General Fiction
Non Fiction and Westerns

Special interest titles available in large print are:
The Little Oxford Dictionary
Music Book, Song Book
Hymn Book, Service Book

Also available from us courtesy of Oxford University Press:
Young Readers' Dictionary
(large print edition)
Young Readers' Thesaurus
(large print edition)

For further information or a free brochure, please contact us at:
Ulverscroft Large Print Books Ltd.,
The Green, Bradgate Road, Anstey,
Leicester, LE7 7FU, England.
Tel: (00 44) 0116 236 4325
Fax: (00 44) 0116 234 0205

Other titles in the
Linford Romance Library:

A TENDER CONFLICT

Susan Udy

Believing a local meadow to be the site of an ancient battle, Kristin Lacey and her small band of eco-protesters set up camp there in order to fend off ruthless property developer Daniel Hunter and his plans for 'executive' homes. Then Kristin discovers her mother has a secret that could put a spanner in the works — and, to make matters worse, she finds herself increasingly attracted to the very man who should be her enemy. When her feelings betray her, is she playing straight into his hands?